Contents

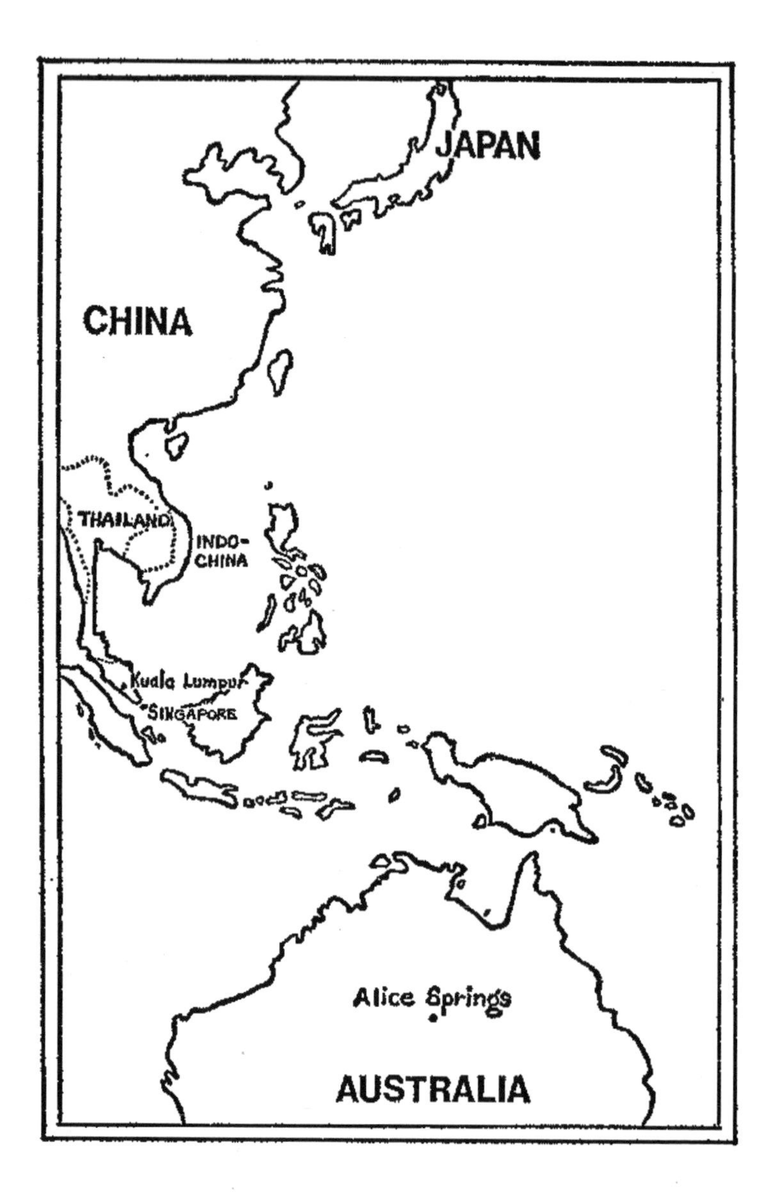
JAPAN
CHINA
THAILAND
INDO-
CHINA
Kuala Lumpur
SINGAPORE
Alice Springs
AUSTRALIA

1

Jean's Early Life

Jean Paget was born in Malaya, in 1921. At that time Malaya was ruled by the British and many people from Britain lived and worked in Malaya. Some of them were government officers, others were in the army and the police force, and others worked in schools and hospitals. But most British people in Malaya worked in trade and industry. The most important industries were mining tin and growing rubber.

Jean Paget's father was the manager of a large rubber estate[1]. The estate was in the State of Perak, about 100 miles north of the capital city, Kuala Lumpur.

Mr Paget lived on the rubber estate with his wife and family. There were two children, a boy called Donald and a girl called Jean. Donald was three years older than Jean.

When the children were very small, they were looked after by an amah[2]. This amah was a Malay woman and she spoke to them in Malay. And so the children learned to speak both Malay and English.

At first, Mrs Paget taught the children herself. But when Donald was thirteen, he had to go to school in England. Jean was only ten at that time, but she went back to England as well. The two children went to stay with their grandparents near Southampton, a large town about eighty miles from London.

Two years later, the grandparents became ill and Mrs Paget had to go back to England. She bought a small house in Southampton and lived there with the children.

When Jean was thirteen, her father was killed in a car accident. He had gone to Kuala Lumpur to do some business and it was late at night when he set out on his journey home.

Probably he was tired and fell asleep in the car. The car left the road and hit a tree. Mr Paget was killed.

Mrs Paget did not have to worry about the future. The company paid her a pension[3] and they also promised to give Donald a job when he left school.

Jean and Donald were quite ordinary children. They were not very clever, but they worked hard and did well at school. There was one thing unusual about them – they were able to speak Malay. At first, they did this as a joke and as a secret family language. If they spoke in Malay, no one else could understand them.

Later, however, they had a very good reason for speaking Malay. Donald wanted to go back to Malaya, to work for the rubber company. His ability to speak Malay would be useful. And so it was important for him not to forget the language. He practised it at home, and Jean practised it with him.

Donald went back to Malaya in 1937, when Jean was sixteen. She left school the following year and went to a commercial college in Southampton. She studied shorthand and typing for six months and then she worked for a year as a shorthand typist in an office. During the year, her mother made arrangements for her to go out to Malaya.

Mrs Paget wrote to the chairman of the rubber company for whom Donald was working. She knew that the company needed secretaries in their offices in Kuala Lumpur. She suggested that Jean might work for the company, as well as Donald.

The company were pleased with Donald's work and they agreed to employ his sister. Jean spoke Malay. It would be very useful for the company to have a secretary who could work in both English and Malay. They wrote back to Mrs Paget straightaway and offered Jean a job.

This was the year 1939 and suddenly, in September, Germany invaded Poland and the Second World War began. The war did not make Jean change her plans. In fact, she thought that Malaya would be a safe place. All the fighting was in Europe.

Fortunately, there was very little fighting at the beginning of the war. Jean was able to get a ship and leave England without any difficulty. She arrived in Malaya in December 1939.

Jean loved her life in Malaya. She lived in Kuala Lumpur and she had a room in a small private hotel which was owned by an Englishwoman. All the people living in the hotel were English and most of them were girls who worked in offices.

Jean's office was in the centre of the city. She liked her work and made a lot of friends. She worked hard in the mornings. In the afternoons, she played tennis and in the evenings, she went to parties and dances. There was always something enjoyable to do.

Jean's future seemed certain. One day she would get married. She would marry a man who worked in a tin mine or on a rubber estate. And she would live in Malaya, as her mother had done. She would have a very happy life.

It would be very like living in England. But the weather would always be warm and sunny and there would be lots of servants to help her with the housework. Jean seemed to be a very lucky girl.

But then everything changed. In 1941, Japan entered the war on the side of Germany.

2

Jean Leaves Kuala Lumpur

Japan invaded Manchuria and attacked China and Indo-China. The Japanese planned to conquer those countries first. After that, they planned to invade Malaya and countries further south, as far as Australia and New Zealand.

The British people in Malaya did not believe that the Japanese were strong enough to defeat so many countries. In Kuala Lumpur, the British continued to work and to go to parties in the same way as before. Some of the young men joined a volunteer army[4] and did army training two or three times a week. But that was a pleasant difference. When they went to parties, they wore their new uniforms and they felt very smart.

Before long the Japanese invaded Malaya on the north-east coast, near a town called Kota Bahru. Kota Bahru was over 300 miles away from Kuala Lumpur. There were steep mountains and thick jungle between the Japanese army and the capital. The people in Kuala Lumpur felt safe.

Two battleships were sent from England to fight the Japanese. They were soon sunk by Japanese aeroplanes. Then the government in Kuala Lumpur asked the women and children to leave for Singapore, 200 miles to the south. Only a few women and children left for Singapore. Jean and many others remained behind. They did not believe that they were in danger.

The Japanese moved quickly south. They used aeroplanes to fly their soldiers across the mountains. When the soldiers landed, they used any lorries, cars and bicycles that they found on the way.

At last, the British people in Kuala Lumpur realised that they were in great danger. One morning, Jean's boss, Mr Merriman, called Jean into his office.

'Jean,' he said. 'I've got some bad news for you. The Japs are in Ipoh, only 100 miles from here. There isn't any time to lose. We're closing the office today, and we want you to get to the station as quickly as you can. Take the first train to Singapore.'

'Singapore?' asked Jean in surprise. 'But what will I do there? Where will I go?'

'Go to our office in Singapore,' replied Mr Merriman. 'The people there will look after you. They'll get you a place on a ship and you'll be able to sail back home to England.'

'It's really dangerous here, then?' asked Jean.

'Really dangerous,' replied Mr Merriman. 'I've already told all the other girls. You'll find them at the station and you'll be able to go with them.'

Jean left the office and walked straight to her bank. She took out all her money, which was about 600 dollars. Then she went to her hotel and packed her things in a suitcase. She left the hotel and began to walk to the railway station.

Suddenly, she remembered some friends who lived twenty miles to the north of the city. She was sure they had not left yet. They would be glad of her help on the long journey south. So she did not catch a train, but got on a bus going north to Batu Tasik.

Jean's friends were called Bill and Eileen Holland. Bill was the manager of a tin mine. He lived in a nice bungalow beside the mine with his wife, Eileen, and their three children. They had two boys, Freddie and Robin, and a girl called Jane. Freddie was the eldest and he was seven years old. Jane was four and Robin was only ten months old and still a baby.

Jean arrived at Batu Tasik about midday. Eileen Holland was alone with the children. Everything was in a muddle. There were lots of suitcases and bags lying on the floor and clothes were scattered everywhere. Freddie had been playing in the garden and his clothes and feet were covered with mud. Jane had fallen down and cut her knee. She was crying. The baby was crying as well, because he was hungry. Eileen was trying to cook some lunch and look after them all. When she saw Jean, she smiled.

'Jean, dear, I'm so glad to see you,' said Eileen. 'There's so much to do and everything's in such a muddle. And the children are hungry.'

'You get lunch ready,' replied Jean. 'I'll look after the children.'

Jean began at once. She put a small plaster on Jane's knee and washed Freddie's feet and legs. Then she found some clean clothes for him. Very soon lunch was ready and they sat down to eat.

'Where's Bill?' asked Jean.

'In KL[5],' Eileen replied. 'He went this morning to buy new tyres for our old car. We haven't used it for a long time. The engine works, but two of the tyres are nearly worn out.'

'What about the cars and lorries that belong to the company?' asked Jean. 'Why don't you take one of them?'

'They've all gone,' said Eileen. 'The army took them all a few weeks ago. The old car was the only one they left.'

'When did Bill leave?' asked Jean.

'Early this morning,' replied Eileen. 'He's been away for eight hours now. I'm getting worried.'

'He'll be all right,' replied Jean. 'He'll be back soon.'

'I feel much happier with you here,' said Eileen. 'Will you stay and help us?'

'Of course,' replied Jean.

It was nearly dark when Bill Holland came back. He was hot and tired, but he was pleased to see Jean. He sat down and had a long drink of cold water.

'I had to walk the last five miles,' he told them. 'The bus wouldn't go any further. It was terribly hot walking.'

'Have you got the tyres?' Eileen asked him.

'No, Eileen,' he replied. 'I haven't. The army have taken every tyre in KL. I couldn't find any.'

'Then what are we going to do?' asked Eileen.

'There's a bus leaving for Singapore at eight o'clock tomorrow,' Bill replied. 'You'll all be able to get seats on that bus, so you'll be all right. You'll be in Singapore by this time tomorrow.'

'But how are we going to get to KL?' Eileen asked.

'In the car,' Bill replied. 'We'll have to use the old tyres. It's only twenty miles. If we drive slowly and carefully, we'll get there all right.'

'Why don't we start this evening?' said Jean.

'That's a good idea,' Eileen agreed. 'It's much cooler at night and the children can sleep in the car.'

'We can't leave tonight,' answered Bill. 'It isn't safe. The army won't let anyone use the roads at night. They've put sentries[6] at all the bridges and crossroads. They'll shoot anyone they see.'

'Things are getting worse and worse,' said Jean. 'We'll have to leave early tomorrow. Let's get everything packed now. Then there won't be so much to do in the morning.'

'What time will we get up?' asked Eileen.

'About four o'clock,' said Bill. 'That'll give us time to dress the children and have some breakfast. Then we can load the car, lock up the house and leave early.'

'Right,' said Jean. 'Let's start packing now.'

It was nearly midnight when they got to bed. Jean was very tired, but she could not sleep properly. In the middle of the night, she heard Bill Holland get up and go outside. She watched him through her mosquito net[7]. He was standing still and looking towards the forest. She climbed out of bed and walked along the verandah[8] towards him.

'What's the matter?' she asked.

'I thought I heard something,' replied Bill.

'Near the house?' she whispered.

'No. I thought I heard guns firing a long way away,' he answered. 'But I can't hear anything now.'

They stood still and listened, but the only sound was the noise of frogs and insects.

'I wish it was morning,' said Bill.

They went back to bed. During the night, the Japanese soldiers slipped past the British soldiers and reached Slim River. They were now less than fifty miles away.

3

The Journey to Kuala Panong

Bill, Eileen and Jean got up two hours before dawn. They packed the suitcases and loaded them into the car. They made breakfast and woke the children. By the time it was light, they were ready to go.

The car was dangerously full. It was loaded with three adults[9], three children and a lot of luggage. Bill drove slowly and carefully, so that he would not damage the old tyres. But one of the tyres burst, after only two miles.

They had to use the spare tyre, which was even older. Everyone got out of the car and watched Bill change the wheel. It did not take him long and after ten minutes they started off again.

Bill drove even more carefully than before, but it was no use.

Everyone got out of the car and watched Bill change the wheel.

After another half mile, the spare tyre burst too. Bill decided to keep on driving, on the rim[10] of the wheel. It was very bad for the car, but there was nothing else he could do. The wheel lasted for two more miles. Then it broke and the car could go no further.

They were still about fifteen miles from Kuala Lumpur and it was seven o'clock. The bus for Singapore would leave in an hour's time. They could still catch it, but only if they found another car at once.

Not far from the road, there were some houses which belonged to a rubber estate. Eileen and Jean stayed in the car with the children. Bill ran to see if he could get any help. First, he tried to find the manager, but he found no one. Then he looked for a car or a lorry, but the army had taken them all. He walked slowly back to his car, wondering what to do next.

When he got back, he found the children crying and everyone feeling very hot and thirsty.

'I couldn't find anything,' he said. 'We'll have to walk.'

'Let's go back to the bungalow,' said Eileen. 'It's cooler there and we'll be more comfortable. This heat is terrible and we haven't got enough to drink.'

'But it's five miles back to the bungalow,' said Bill. 'Let's walk towards KL. We might meet a lorry and get a lift.'

'But perhaps we won't see a lorry,' said Eileen. 'What will we do then? We can't walk fifteen miles.'

'What do you think, Jean?' Bill asked.

'We can't stay here,' Jean replied. 'And I'm sure that we can't walk all the way to KL. I agree with Eileen. I think we should go back to the bungalow.'

So they went back. They left the luggage in the car and locked all the doors. Each adult carried one child and they started to walk back to the bungalow.

They reached home at midday, very tired and thirsty. After some iced drinks from the fridge, they all lay down on their beds.

An hour later, a lorry drove up and stopped outside the

bungalow. Jean woke up and went out to see who it was. A young army officer jumped out and came hurrying over towards her.

'What are you doing here?' he asked. 'You'll have to leave with me in the lorry at once. How many of you are there?'

'Six,' said Jean. 'Three adults and three children.'

'But what about our luggage?' asked Eileen, who had come outside with Bill.

'Yes,' said Bill. 'All our luggage is in the car. And the car is about six miles away, on the KL road. Can't you take us there first?'

'No, I can't,' said the officer firmly. 'The Japs are only twenty miles away; I'm going to take you to Panong. With luck, you'll find a boat there to take you to Singapore.'

So the Hollands and Jean climbed onto the back of the lorry. The army officer drove round the tin mines and rubber estates and picked up all the British people. They reached Panong in the middle of the afternoon, with about forty men, women and children in the back of the lorry. Some of them had not known they were in danger and had not tried to get away. Others, like the Hollands, had tried to leave, but had been too late.

The officer drove the lorry right up to the District Commissioner's[11] office. He left everyone sitting in the lorry and went inside. After a few minutes, the D.C. came outside to look at the lorry and its load of people. He looked very worried.

'Drive the lorry to the accounts office, over there,' he told the officer. 'The passengers can get off and sit on the verandah for an hour or two. Tell them not to walk too far away.'

'Have you got a motorboat?' the officer asked him.

'No, I haven't,' replied the D.C.

'Then how will you get them away?' the officer asked.

'I don't know,' the D.C. replied. 'I hope I can send them down the coast in fishing boats. There are some in the harbour, over there.'

The officer drove over to the accounts office and everyone got off the lorry. They were pleased to move about again and to be out of the sun, in the shade of the verandah.

Eileen sat down with her back against a wall and the children played beside her. Bill and Jean walked to the shops. They had left everything in the car and now they had nothing with them.

They were able to buy a little food and some medicine. They looked for mosquito nets, but they did not find any. Jean bought some needle and thread for herself. She noticed a large canvas haversack[12] and bought that, as well. She did not know it at the time, but she was going to carry that haversack for the next three years.

They got back to the verandah about tea-time and showed Eileen what they had bought. After a small meal of biscuits and lemonade, they sat and waited.

Meanwhile, the D.C. had been trying to get boats for them. Towards sunset, he received a telephone call from one of the men in the lighthouse[13]. There was good news. The *Osprey*, a large motorboat, was coming up the river.

The D.C. did not know why the *Osprey* was coming up the river. But it was big and fast and could take all the refugees[14] down the coast. He decided to speak to the captain as soon as the boat arrived. He left his office and walked down to the harbour.

Soon, the *Osprey* came round the bend in the river. The D.C. could see a great many soldiers on board. They were short men and wore grey-green uniforms. They were Japanese.

The D.C. felt a great sadness. The Japanese had captured the *Osprey* and soon would capture all the refugees. He could do nothing to help them.

4

Prisoners

The Japanese soldiers jumped quickly onto the land. Immediately, they arrested the D.C. They held their guns against his back and made him walk up to the office.

The Japanese expected to find some British soldiers at Panong, but there were no soldiers there. Even the army officer who had driven the lorry had gone off to look for more people.

The Japanese soldiers soon came to the accounts office, where they found the British families. The Japanese made them prisoners at once, and ordered the women to hand over their rings and watches. The soldiers took the watches and jewellery and went away.

About an hour later, a Japanese officer came to the office. Two soldiers came with him and made the prisoners stand in a line. They pointed their rifles at the prisoners. The children were frightened and began to cry. None of the prisoners knew what would happen.

The officer looked at them for a few minutes. Then he spoke to them in broken English[15].

'You now prisoners,' he said. 'You obey me and my soldiers. If not obey, my soldiers shoot you.'

Nobody said anything.

'You stay here tonight,' he said. 'Tomorrow, you go to prison camp.'

'Can we have beds and mosquito nets?' asked one of the men.

'Japanese soldiers not have beds and mosquito nets,' he told them. 'Prisoners same as soldiers. No beds. No mosquito nets.'

'Can we have some food?' asked another man.

'Food tomorrow,' he replied. 'Now sleep.'

The officer left the soldiers to guard the prisoners and went away.

The prisoners got ready to sleep on the floor of the verandah. Although they were very tired, they could not sleep well. The floor was hard and the mosquitoes bit them terribly. All through the night the children woke up crying because their arms and legs were sore. The adults had to get up and look after the children. When they lay down again, they thought about what might happen to them. They were too worried to sleep.

When morning came, all the prisoners were feeling miserable. Few of them had slept at all. Their arms and legs were swollen with mosquito bites and their bodies were stiff and sore. They felt very dirty, but there was no water to wash in.

They did not get any food, so they used the food that they had brought with them. The Hollands were quite lucky, because Jean and Bill had bought some food the day before. After eating something, everyone felt a little better.

In the middle of the morning, Captain Yoniata, the Japanese officer, asked them all questions. He spoke to each family in turn and wrote down the answers in a school exercise book. The questions did not take long. Afterwards, Captain Yohiata spoke to them.

'Men go to prison camp today,' he said. 'Women and children stay here. Men go this afternoon. Now say goodbye.'

They were all sad when they heard this. The adults knew that in war, men and women usually went into different camps. But they had hoped that they would be together for a little longer.

While the families were getting ready to say goodbye, Jean tried to get some ointment to keep off the mosquitoes. First, she went up to one of the guards. She pointed to her mosquito bites and then to the shops. The guard pointed his rifle at her and pushed her back onto the verandah. She had to think of another way of getting some ointment.

Next, she went to the back of the office. Some village children were playing about fifty metres away. She waved to them and called softly in Malay.

'Girl, you, girl,' she called. 'Come here.'

A child came towards her. She was about twelve years old.

'What is your name?' asked Jean.

'Halijah,' replied the girl shyly[16].

'Now, Halijah, do you know the shop that sells medicines?' Jean said quietly. 'The Chinese shop in the village over there?'

'I know it,' said Halijah at once. 'It is Chan Kok Fuan's shop.'

'Good,' said Jean. 'Go to Chan Kok Fuan and tell him to come to me. Tell him that the white prisoners have mosquito bites and want to buy some medicines. If he comes, I'll give you ten cents.'

The child went off, and soon the Chinese shopkeeper came with a basket of ointments. He went up to the sentry and pointed to the prisoners. The sentry let him go onto the verandah. Jean bought six tubes of ointment and the other women quickly bought the rest. Halijah got her ten cents.

Later, a Japanese soldier brought two buckets of watery fish soup and another bucket, half filled with dirty boiled rice. The prisoners did not have any bowls and did not share the food out carefully. Some had too much and some did not have any at all. But there were still some biscuits and those who were hungry ate them.

In the afternoon, Captain Yoniata returned with several soldiers. He ordered the men to get ready at once. The men said goodbye to their wives and children. Bill Holland asked Jean to help Eileen with the three children. Then the men were made to stand in a line and march away.

There were thirty-two prisoners left in the camp. Nineteen were children. The eldest child was fourteen, and the youngest was still a baby. All the women were married, except two, Jean and another girl. Jean was the only one who could speak Malay.

The child went off, and soon the Chinese shopkeeper came with a basket of ointments.

They were going to stay in the accounts office for forty-one days.

That evening, they got another bucket of fish soup, so they were not so hungry that night. They were a little more comfortable, because they were allowed to use the rooms inside the office. But there were still no mosquito nets or blankets or beds and the prisoners did not sleep very well.

Next morning, one of the women asked to see the captain. Her name was Mrs Horsefall. When he came, she spoke angrily.

'Captain Yoniata,' she said. 'We can't sleep here, like this. We must have beds. We must have blankets. We must have mosquito nets.'

'No beds, no mosquito nets,' Captain Yoniata replied. 'Japanese women not have beds. You same as Japanese women.'

'But we're British,' said Mrs Horsefall angrily. 'We aren't animals. We don't sleep on the floor.'

Captain Yoniata looked fiercely at her. He ordered two soldiers to hold her arms. Then he hit her four times across the face.

'Bad woman!' he shouted, and then he walked away.

When Captain Yoniata came to inspect[17] them, next morning, Mrs Horsefall bravely spoke to him again. This time, she asked him for water to wash in. He agreed to send some each day. After that, they were able to keep themselves clean, but they still could not wash their clothes.

At first, the prisoners had some money and were able to buy things that they needed. Most families ordered one cooked meal each day from the restaurant, because they did not like the fish soup and rice. They got soap from the shops and quinine, a medicine which kept them free from malaria.

Slowly, they got used to their new way of life. The children did not mind sleeping on the floor, but it was much more difficult for the older women. They could never sleep for more than half an hour, without waking up in pain. But they did sleep a little.

At the end of the first week, most of the prisoners got dysentery[18]. All through the night, children were carried, crying, to the toilet. Captain Yoniata tried to help. He increased the ice ration[19] and brought the prisoners a bucket of tea every afternoon.

On the thirty-fifth day, one girl died. She was only eight. She had had dysentery for some time and she had grown weaker and weaker. She slept very little and cried a great deal. Then she got a fever and, for two days, she had a temperature of 40°C. Mrs Horsefall told Captain Yoniata that the girl must have a doctor, but there were no doctors in Panong. Next morning, the little girl died and she was buried that day.

At the end of six weeks, Captain Yoniata spoke to the prisoners after the morning inspection. Their clothes were torn and dirty. Many of the adults and most of the children were ill.

'Ladies,' he said. 'The armies of the Emperor of Japan now in Singapore. All Malaya now free. Prison camps for women and children in Singapore. You go to Singapore. In Singapore you happy.'

'How do we get to Singapore?' asked Mrs Horsefall.

'You go by train from Kuala Lumpur,' said Captain Yoniata.

'How do we get to Kuala Lumpur?' asked Mrs Horsefall. 'By lorry?'

'Very sorry. No lorry. You walk,' said Captain Yoniata.

'We can't walk that far,' said Mrs Horsefall. 'It's nearly fifty miles. We must have a lorry.'

'No lorry. You walk,' said Captain Yoniata, getting angry.

'But what about our luggage?' asked Mrs Horsefall.

'You carry luggage,' the captain shouted, and he walked away.

At the end of six weeks, Captain Yoniata spoke to the prisoners after the morning inspection.

5

The Road to Kuala Lumpur

At dawn, a soldier brought a bucket of rice and a bucket of tea. The women and children had breakfast and began to get ready for the journey. They took a long time. They were still not ready at nine o'clock when Captain Yoniata came. He was angry to find that they had not left.

'You walk now,' he shouted at them. 'If not, my men beat you. Today you go to Ayer Penchis. Not many miles. If you walk, you happy. If you stay, soldiers beat you. Walk now.'

The thirty-one women and children set off. A Japanese sergeant[20] led the way and three soldiers followed at the back. Eileen Holland carried the baby and Jean's haversack. Jean carried the blankets, which were the heaviest and hottest load, and she led four-year-old Jane by the hand.

They went very slowly. They had to stop every few minutes for someone, and the guards never let anyone get behind. They only walked about one and a half miles each hour.

As the day went on, their feet began to hurt. The children were all right, because they did not have any shoes. The women wore shoes and their feet swelled in the heat. After a while, Jean saw that the children were more comfortable, and so she kicked her shoes off. The road felt hot against her skin, but she could walk more easily.

They reached Ayer Penchis shortly before dark. There was a long building in the village that was used for storing rubber. It was empty and the headman[21] of the village let them stay in it. The Japanese soldiers cooked some tea and rice and fish soup, but most of the prisoners could not eat anything.

Before it was dark, Jean went outside and went up to one of the soldiers. She pointed to the shops in the village and he let her go to them. There were mangoes[22] outside one of the shops and Jean bought some. She ate one at once and felt much better.

Jean went back and gave the other mangoes to Eileen and the children. Some of the mothers gave Jean money to buy more. She went to the village again and this time she bought fifty. Soon, all the children were covered in mango. When the soldiers brought a second bucket of tea, the prisoners gave them a mango each, as a present. After the fruit and the tea, most of the women and children could eat some rice and they felt better.

They woke next morning, stiff and sore. Some of the children had been bitten by rats. It did not seem possible for them to walk further, but the sergeant forced them onto the road.

That day they had to walk only ten miles, to a place called Asahan, but they took all day to get there. One of the older women, called Mrs Collard, had to stop every ten minutes. She was a heavy woman and had become very weak from malaria and dysentery. Now she could hardly walk. Other women carried her load and helped her along the road. The soldiers helped to carry some of their children.

During the afternoon, Mrs Collard's face turned blue and then red. She began to find it difficult to breathe. When they reached Asahan, they found another empty rubber store. Two of the women helped Mrs Collard into the building and she sat down against a wall. One of the women brought water and bathed her face. Then she asked them to wash her two boys, Ben and Harry. When the women came back, Mrs Collard had fallen over and was unconscious[23]. She died a few hours later.

After Mrs Collard had died, Mrs Horsefall and Jean went to see the Japanese sergeant. It was very difficult to make him understand them, so they used signs while they were speaking.

'Tomorrow we can't walk,' they said. 'We must stay here and rest. Today one woman has died. Tomorrow we rest. Next day we will walk again.'

She was a heavy woman and had become very weak. Now she could hardly walk.

'Tomorrow we put woman in earth,' the sergeant replied. 'Next day we walk.'

They buried Mrs Collard early in the morning. The headman of the village showed them where to dig a grave and they put Mrs Collard gently into it. Mrs Horsefall read some words from her prayer book. Afterwards, Jean got a carpenter to put a small, wooden cross over the grave. They could not do anything more.

At about midday, Captain Yoniata arrived in a large motor-car. He was very angry to see the prisoners sitting outside the rubber store.

'Why you not walk?' he asked them angrily. 'You not get food. You walk now.'

'Mrs Collard died last night,' Mrs Horsefall told him. 'We buried her this morning. Her grave is over there. We cannot walk today. We'll walk tomorrow.'

'Why woman die? Malaria?' asked Captain Yoniata.

'She had dysentery and malaria,' Mrs Horsefall answered. 'She was very weak. After walking so far, she was tired and could not breathe. Last night she died. Two other women are so weak today that they cannot stand. Come inside and see them.'

Captain Yoniata went into the building and looked at the two women. They were sitting on the floor, with their backs against the wall. Then Captain Yoniata spoke to Mrs Horsefall in a kinder voice.

'I go to Kuala Lumpur,' he said. 'I get lorry. Very sad woman die.'

The women became much more cheerful. They thought that they would be in Kuala Lumpur next day. But when Captain Yoniata returned in the evening, he brought bad news.

'You cannot go to Kuala Lumpur. No bridges for trains. English break all bridges. You go now to Port Swettenham. You get boat to Singapore,' he told them.

'What about the lorry?' Mrs Horsefall asked.

'Very sorry, no lorries,' he replied. 'You must walk. You walk slowly. Two days or three days. Then you get boat.'

'But that's impossible, Captain,' said Mrs Horsefall. 'We can't walk that far. We must have a lorry for the children.'

'No lorries,' he repeated. 'You walk.' Captain Yoniata said no more. He got into his car and drove off. They never saw him again.

6

The Journey to Klang

The next morning, they started their journey again. Now there were only two soldiers to help carry the children. Captain Yoniata had taken the other two soldiers away, because he was sure that no one could escape.

Mrs Holland was walking so badly that Jean carried the baby, as well as the blankets. Jean still walked barefoot and led Jane by the hand. Eileen Holland carried the haversack and looked after Freddie.

That night, they stayed at a bungalow near a village called Bakri. There was a bath and a pile of firewood for heating water. Everyone had a hot bath and the women washed their clothes. They enjoyed this and felt much happier. Soon, they thought, they would be on a ship.

The next day, they walked in the shade through some rubber plantations. It was difficult to find the way. Jean asked the rubber workers in Malay and then she pointed the way to the sergeant.

In the afternoon, one of the boys stepped on a scorpion[24] in the long grass. It was Ben Collard, the youngest son of the woman who had died. He was stung in the foot and he was in great pain. His foot swelled up so much that he could not walk at all. Mrs Horsefall carried him for an hour and then the sergeant carried him for the rest of the way.

They stopped, that night, at a village called Dilit. The sergeant asked the headman for food and shelter. The headman did not want them to stay in the village. All the houses were full and the Japanese could not give him any money for the food. After some time, the headman gave them some rice and fish and let them use one small hut. The sergeant promised that the headman would be paid later.

As soon as they were inside the hut, the women tried to help Ben. They cut open his foot with a razor and rubbed some medicine into it. Then they covered it with hot bandages. While they were doing this, Jean walked over to the headman and spoke to him.

'I'm sorry that we've caused you so much trouble,' she said.

'It's no trouble,' he replied. 'We're sorry to see you all so ill and tired. Have you come far?'

'From Bakri today,' Jean told him.

The headman invited her into the house. They drank a cup of coffee and Jean told him what had happened to them.

'The Japanese sergeant says you must stay here tomorrow,' the headman said.

'We are too weak to march each day,' said Jean. 'The soldiers allow us to rest a day between marching. If we stay here tomorrow, it will help us. The sergeant says he can get money for food.'

'The Japanese never pay for food,' said the old man, 'but you can stay here.'

'I can do nothing except thank you,' said Jean.

The headman smiled and said, 'In the fourth Surah of the

The women tried to help Ben.

Koran[25], it says, "God is pleased if you are kind to women and help them." '

They rested all next day at Dilit and then set out for Klang, about four miles outside Port Swettenham. Little Ben Collard was now very weak. His foot was still swollen and painful and he had not been able to eat or sleep. As soon as he ate anything, he was sick. The headman told the villagers to make a stretcher[26] for him. The women put him onto the stretcher and carried him the rest of the way.

When they got to Klang, the sergeant put them in an empty school house. Then he went to look for the officer in charge and get some food. Soon, he returned with an officer called Major Nemu, who spoke good English.

'Who are you?' he asked them. 'What do you want?'

'We're prisoners,' Mrs Horsefall answered. 'We've come from Panong. We were sent by Captain Yoniata. He said a ship would take us to prison in Singapore.'

'There are no ships here,' Major Nemu said. 'You should have stayed in Panong.'

'We were sent here,' Mrs Horsefall said again. She decided to talk about something else. 'Is there a doctor here? Some of us are ill and one child is in great pain. One woman died on the way.'

'What did she die of?' Major Nemu asked quickly. 'Was it a disease?'

'No, it wasn't. She died because of walking. The boy was bitten by a scorpion,' answered Mrs Horsefall.

'I'll send a doctor,' Major Nemu said. 'You can stay here tonight, but you can't stay for long. I haven't got enough food for my own men. I can't possibly feed another thirty people as well.'

He went back to his camp. Later that day, a doctor came to visit them. He told the women to continue putting hot bandages on Ben's foot and went away. But Ben got worse. Three days later, they sent for the doctor again and persuaded him to put the child into hospital. On the sixth day, they heard that he had died.

7

The March to the East Coast

They stayed at Klang for eleven days. The food was poor and they were given very little. They had spent nearly all their money, so they could not buy anything extra to eat.

On the twelfth day, Major Nemu came to inspect them. He put a corporal[27] in charge of them, instead of the sergeant. The major ordered them to walk to Port Dickson. There might be a boat there which could take them to Singapore. He did not want them in Klang any longer.

It was now the middle of March, 1942, and they did not reach Port Dickson until the end of the month. They had to wait several days in one village because Mrs Horsefall had a bad fever. She had a temperature of 40°C for three days. When she recovered, she could hardly walk. She slowly got stronger, but she was never the same again. From then on, Jean became the leader of the group.

By the time they reached Port Dickson, their clothes were dirty and badly torn. Jean sold a brooch[28] for thirteen dollars and used two dollars to buy a length of cloth. With the cloth, she made a sarong – a simple, Malay dress. She made a blouse out of the top of her old dress. After that, she was much more comfortable. Later, some of the other women did the same.

They did not find a boat at Port Dickson, but it was quite a good place to stay. They could swim in the sea and the sea water helped the sores on their skin. But after ten days the Japanese commander made them move on again. He told them to go to Seremban and get a train there.

On the way to Seremban, young Jane Holland died. She got malaria and they could only bathe her head and keep her still. Two days later she died and they buried her in a Muslim[29] cemetery. Eileen Holland was very calm during that sad day, but Jean heard her weeping through most of the night.

Robin, the baby, was doing well, and by now he was very brown. He never got dysentery, as the others did. Jean looked after him for most of the time and carried him during the marches. She had had an attack of fever herself in Klang, but quickly recovered and was growing fitter and stronger.

There were no trains at Seremban. They were told to walk south to Tampin. At Tampin, they were told to walk to Malacca and get on a boat. At Malacca, there were no boats and they were told to go back to Tampin. There was so little food at Tampin that the women asked if they could walk on south, towards Singapore.

The next town was Gemas. On the way there, Mrs Horsefall died. She had never recovered fully from the fever she had had two months before. She often had a high temperature and grew very weak. At Ayer Kuning, she got dysentery badly and died two days later. Mrs Frith said she would look after Mrs Horsefall's son, Johnny.

Mrs Frith was over fifty and the oldest member of the group. On the long march, she had complained more than anyone else. Several times she had been so ill that everyone expected her to die. Now she suddenly changed and became very active and helpful, especially to Jean. She had lived in Malaya for fifteen years and had visited most parts of the country.

When they reached Gemas, they were put into an empty school house. As usual, the corporal went to find the local commander and arrange for food. He returned with the officer in charge. Jean explained to him who they were and why they had come.

'We want to get to Singapore and to the prison camps there,' she said finally.

'No more prisoners in Singapore,' said Captain Nitsui.

'But where can we go?' asked Jean sadly. 'We can't go on walking. Seven of us have died already. We must get into a camp.

'Very sorry. You can't go to Singapore,' Captain Nitsui said firmly. 'Too many prisoners in Singapore.'

'Can we stay here, then[7]' asked Jean.

'No. No,' shouted Captain Nitsui.

'Then where can we go?' Jean asked.

'I tell you tomorrow,' he replied and went away.

Jean told the women what the Captain had said. They were not very surprised.

'If they left us alone, we could find a village and stay there till the war is over,' said Mrs Frith.

'That would be the best thing,' Jean agreed. 'But the village couldn't feed us. The Japs give us food.'

'They don't give us very much food,' said Mrs Frith. 'We nearly starved[30] at Tampin.'

Next morning, the Japanese officer came back and spoke to them all.

'Today you start journey to Kuantan. New camp for women there,' he told them.

'Kuantan? Where is that?' asked one of the women.

'On the east coast, about 150 miles away,' Mrs Frith said.

'Can we go there by train?' asked Jean.

'Very sorry. No trains,' the Captain answered.

'Can we go there by lorry?' she asked.

'Very sorry. No lorries,' Captain Nitsui replied. 'You walk.

Few miles each day. Very nice journey. You be happy at Kuantan. Now you go.'

'We can't go now,' Jean said firmly. 'We aren't ready and we haven't had any breakfast yet.'

'Tonight I send you good meal. Tomorrow you walk early,' Captain Nitsui said, and he walked away.

The women discussed what they should do.

'I don't believe there's a prison camp at Kuantan,' said one woman.

'I don't either,' said another. 'They don't want us anywhere. We eat food and we cause trouble, so each officer sends us somewhere else.'

'Well, Kuantan's a better place to go to,' said Mrs Frith. 'It's nice on the east coast. It's much more healthy there and the people are kinder.'

In the morning, they started off with a sergeant and a different soldier. They had to walk along the railway. There were no trains, so it was not dangerous. It was very hot, because there were no trees overhead to give shade.

They went on for a week, resting every other day. Then fever broke out among the children. All of them got the fever at one time or another. Seven children had it at a place called Bahau. They stayed there for a week, living in the railway station. Although the women did their best to help the children, four of them died and one of them was Freddie Holland.

After Freddie's death, Jean was worried about Eileen. She tried to make her take more interest in the baby, Robin, but Eileen was too weak to carry him. Jean continued to carry Robin and play with him. Eileen gave him his food.

The Japanese soldiers helped them quite a lot. Each of them usually carried one child and held one handle of the stretcher. They could speak to the women only by signs. Jean spoke for them at the villages and found out the way for them.

At Ayer Kring, Eileen Holland came to the end of her strength. She had fallen twice that day and been helped along by the women. Although she was now much thinner, she was too heavy to carry on the stretcher. She managed to reach the village of Ayer Kring that night, but she was changing colour. Her face turned a deep red and then blue.

They found a house for her to rest in. The women bathed her face and gave her a little soup. She refused to eat anything and knew that she would die soon. She whispered to Jean during the night.

'I'm so sorry to make trouble for you, my dear,' she said. 'I'm so sorry for Bill. If you see him again, tell him not to be unhappy. Tell him to marry someone else. He's still a young man.'

After a few moments, she spoke again. 'I'm so glad the baby likes you,' she said.

In the morning, she was still alive, but unconscious. Her breathing became weaker and weaker and at about midday she died. They buried her in the village cemetery that evening.

Ayer Kring was a very unhealthy place, full of mosquitoes. The land around it was flat and full of swamps[31]. By day it was hot, and at night a cold mist came up from the swamps.

Nearly everyone began to suffer from another sort of fever. They did not have a high temperature, but they had a terrible headache and felt sick. Jean was ill also and wanted to stop and rest for a day. But the sergeant and Mrs Frith, who was well and cheerful, said they must move out of the swamp, into higher country. Jean agreed and they kept on marching.

Even Robin, the baby, got the fever. It was his first illness. Jean showed him to the headman of one of the villages. The headman's wife brought out a hot drink made from the bark[32] of a tree. Jean tasted it and gave some to Robin, who got better during the night. Others were not so lucky. Three more women and another child died on this part of the journey.

At last, they reached the higher ground and decided to rest for one day. They stopped at a village where the people were kind, and gave them a place to sleep and plenty of fruit and vegetables. Jean and the others felt much better after their rest and walked on steadily.

Four days later, they reached the main road which runs from Kuala Lumpur to Kuantan. There was a small town called Merau with about fifty houses, a school and some shops. By the side of the road they found two lorries. Two white men were repairing one of them, while Japanese guards stood by. They were the first white men they had seen for five months.

8

The Australian Lorry Drivers

The small group of women and children walked up to the lorry and watched the men working. The lorry was full of wooden planks, taken from the railway. One Japanese guard was sitting on top of the lorry, holding a rifle. Another was standing on the road, also with a rifle. Neither soldier said anything to the women and they stood and watched. Then one of the white men spoke in English.

'Tell those women to move away,' he shouted. 'I can't see what I'm doing.'

The women laughed. They were pleased to hear English spoken again.

'All right. Don't get angry,' said Jean. 'We're only watching.'

'Who said that?' asked the man. 'Who spoke in English?'

'I did,' said Jean. 'We're all British.'

The two men looked up at them. The women were dressed like Malay women. Jean was wearing her long, black hair in a plait[33] down her back, and she wore no shoes. The children's clothes were all torn and their skins were burnt a deep brown by the sun.

'You don't look British,' the taller man said.

'Perhaps we don't,' said Jean, 'but we are.'

'Where have you come from?' he asked. 'What are you doing here?'

'We're prisoners,' answered Jean. She pointed to the soldier who had come with them. 'We're walking to the prison camp at Kuantan.'

'There isn't a prison camp in Kuantan,' the man said. 'There are only a few prisoners there like us. We all drive lorries. We live in a hut, but there isn't a camp.'

'I'm not surprised,' said Jean. 'The Japs have told us lies all the

The small group of women and children walked up to the lorry and watched the men working.

time. Nobody wants us, so they send us somewhere else.'

'Where have you come from?' the man asked.

'We were taken prisoner in Panong five months ago,' said Mrs Frith. 'We've been to Klang, Port Dickson, Seremban, Tampin, Malacca, Gemas and now here.'

'We've walked about 500 miles,' said Jean.

'500 miles! Have all of you walked that far?' asked the man.

'Yes,' replied Jean. 'All of us and fifteen others who died on the way.'

'What?' said the man in astonishment. 'Fifteen of you have died? Hey, Ben! Do you hear what has happened to them?'

The man's friend was talking to some of the other women. 'These women have been telling me,' he replied. 'I can't believe it.'

'What about you?' asked Jean. 'Who are you and what are you doing here?'

'We're Australians,' said the man. 'I'm Joe Harman and he's Ben Leggatt. We were captured about two months ago and we've been driving lorries ever since. It's much better than being in a prison camp. Where are you staying tonight?'

'Here,' answered Jean. 'We'll have to go and ask the village headman where we can sleep.'

'What will you do tomorrow?' he asked.

'We usually rest one day and walk the next,' she replied. 'We can't make the children walk every day. So we'll stay here. But perhaps we can get a lift on your lorry. What's the matter with it?'

'The brakes caught fire,' Joe answered, 'but we've mended them now. We can easily break something else so that we can stay here another night. What can we do to the lorry, Ben?'

'We can take the back axle[34] off. That'll make a lot of mess and we won't be able to move. I'll get on with that now,' answered Ben.

'OK. I'll help you in a minute,' said Joe.

He turned to Jean. 'How can we help you?' he asked her. 'Have you got any medicines?'

'No, we haven't, and we need some badly,' said Jean. 'We need some for stomach trouble, malaria and skin diseases. Many of the children are very sick.'

'Have you got any money?' Joe asked.

'No, we've spent all our money,' replied Jean. 'But we've still got some small pieces of jewellery, which we can sell.'

'I hope we won't need to use them,' said Joe. 'I'll see what I can find. Get somewhere to sleep and I'll come and see you later.'

Jean went back to the sergeant and, together, they asked the headman for food and shelter. They were allowed to use the school house and soon they were washing and cleaning as usual.

Meanwhile, the two Australians went back to work. After an hour, they had taken off the back axle, which was dripping with oil. They showed it to the guard and told him that they could not move that night. The guard was suspicious[35], but there was nothing he could do. He went away to get some food for them.

Now there was only one soldier guarding them. Joe got up and pretended to go to the toilet. He walked quickly behind a row of houses to some shops. He found a Chinese man who owned a bus and spoke to him in broken English.

'You want petrol?' Joe asked. 'How much money you give?'

After a few minutes of bargaining[36], the Australian wrote down some words on a piece of paper: Medicines – dysentery – malaria – skin diseases. Then the bus owner gave him three empty petrol cans. Joe hid them in a ditch, on his way back to the lorries. The guard saw him returning, but thought he had been to the toilet.

When it was dark, Joe filled the cans with petrol from the lorry's petrol tank. He carried them back to the Chinese man. The Chinese man gave him some medicines and explained what they were. Then Joe went to the school house and stopped outside the open door.

'Where's the lady I talked to this afternoon?' he whispered.

Jean was already asleep, but they woke her up and she went outside.

'Hello, Joe,' she said.

'Hello,' said Joe. 'Tell me, what's your name?'

'Jean Paget.'

'Jean Paget,' repeated Joe. 'I can remember that. Here are the medicines, Jean. This is quinine, for malaria. And this is a Chinese medicine, for dysentery. You take the powder in hot water every four hours. And this is ointment, for the skin.'

'That's wonderful,' she said. 'How much did it all cost?'

'Don't worry about that,' said Joe. 'I paid for it with the Japs' petrol.'

'I hope that they don't find out,' said Jean. 'Will they be angry in Kuantan if you don't get back until tomorrow?'

'No,' said Joe. 'The lorries often break down. They won't be surprised if we're late.'

'Where are you taking all these wooden planks?' asked Jean.

'I don't know,' replied Joe. 'I think the Japs are building another railway somewhere, but I don't know where.'

Jean sat down on the top step of the doorway and Joe sat on the ground, below her.

'Are you a lorry driver in Australia?' Jean asked.

'No, I'm a ringer. I look after cattle, on a station[37] near Wollera. Wollera's about 100 miles from the Springs.'

'Where are the Springs?' asked Jean.

'Alice Springs? You don't know where Alice Springs is?' Joe said. He was surprised that she did not know.

'It's right in the middle of Australia, about half-way between Adelaide and Darwin.'

'I thought it was all desert in the middle of Australia,' said Jean.

'No,' said Joe. 'There's lots of water there. The gardens round people's houses are green all the year round. Most of the Northern Territory is dry, but there's water in the rivers. And even when the rivers are dry, you can dig down into the river bed and find water.'

'How many cattle do you look after?' Jean asked.

'There were about eighteen thousand when I left,' said Joe. 'Sometimes there are more, sometimes less.'

'Eighteen thousand! How big is the station?' asked Jean.

'About 2700 square miles,' Joe replied.

'As big as that!' said Jean in surprise. 'How many of you work there?'

'There's the manager, four ringers and nine workmen,' Joe told her. 'That makes fourteen of us.'

They sat there quietly, for a moment. The Australian thought of his homeland and Jean tried to imagine the huge station with eighteen thousand cattle and fourteen men. England was very different. There, the cities were crowded with people and all the farms were small.

Jean and Joe talked for about an hour. At the end, Joe stood up to go.

'I mustn't stay any longer,' he said.

'Thanks very much for getting us the medicines,' said Jean. She got up, too. 'They'll be a great help.'

'We'll try and get you some more things,' said Joe. 'What else do you need?'

'Soap is the thing we need most,' Jean answered. 'We haven't any at all and we can't get clean.'

'We'll get some soap, if we can,' Joe said. 'I'm sorry to have talked so much about my home and my country. It must have been boring for you.'

'No, it wasn't boring,' Jean said. 'I liked hearing you talk.'

'Goodnight, Jean,' said Joe.

'Goodnight, Joe,' she said.

Jean watched Joe walk away to the lorries, and then she went inside the school house.

9

Some Soap and a Pig

Next morning, Jean showed the medicines to the other women.

'Joe is a nice man, isn't he?' said Mrs Frith. 'I heard you talking with him for a long time last night.'

'He's homesick[38],' said Jean. 'He liked talking about his own country. He's a ringer, you know. He looks after cattle and the station he works on is sixty miles long.'

'Well, he's been a great help to us,' said Mrs Frith. 'And if he likes to talk, you listen. We can't thank him in any other way. I wonder if they'll be able to take us to Kuantan, on those lorries.'

The women and children waited for some time, but the lorries did not come for them. The Australians had asked their guards to take the women and children with them, but the Japanese soldiers had refused.

'Lorries too full,' they said. 'Women and children break lorries. Prisoners walk.'

It took Joe and Ben the whole morning to put back the axle. When they were ready to go, Joe spoke to Ben.

'Talk to the guard a moment, so that he doesn't see what I'm doing,' he said. 'I'm going to loosen a nut, so that the petrol leaks[39]. I took six gallons out of the tank last night. We'll soon

'Talk to the guard a moment, so that he doesn't see what I'm doing,' he said.

run out of petrol and have to stop. Then we can find the leak and show them how we lost the petrol.'

He loosened the nut, and the petrol began to leak slowly out of the pipe. Then they moved off.

The women rested all that day at Merau. They still had fifty-five miles to walk to Kuantan, but the road was good and there were no swamps. The next day, they walked a long way and spent the night at Buan.

They spent the day resting there. They looked out for the lorries, but they did not see them. In the evening, a Malay girl brought them a parcel. Inside it, there were six packets of soap and a letter from Joe.

Dear Jean,

Here is some soap. I'll try to get some more later. We cannot see you, because the Japs won't let us stop. The lorry ran out of petrol, so we are a day late. The Chinese bus owner in Merau says he'll send this packet to you. Look out for us on your way.

Joe Harman

Next day, the women and children walked on to Berkapor. They passed through a number of coconut plantations[40]. One of the women sold a pair of shoes and bought enough green coconuts to give everyone a drink of coconut milk. At Berkapor, they were put into a long shed, used for storing copra. There, they did their washing as usual, using soap for the first time for many weeks.

Shortly before dark, two lorries drove up and Joe and Ben got out. Jean and some of the others went across to speak to them. Their Japanese guards talked to the soldiers who were with the lorries.

'Thank you for the soap,' said Jean. 'We had a marvellous wash last night.'

'So you got the parcel,' said Joe. 'Good. We've got a pig with us this time.'

'A pig?' asked Jean in surprise.

'Yes. A pig ran out into the road,' said Joe. 'I chased it in the lorry and the Jap fired at it with his rifle. He missed six times and wounded it with the seventh shot. I was able to run it over and kill it. We'll have to let the Japs have most of the meat, but there'll be enough for all of you, too.'

That night, the women got a large piece of pig meat. They made it into a soup with the rice.

Later, Joe Harman came over to talk to Jean. She was playing with the baby and Joe watched them both.

'I'm sorry I couldn't get more meat for you,' he said. 'The Japs had to have most of it.'

'It's been wonderful, Joe,' said Jean. 'That's the first good meal we've had since we left Panong. And there's enough meat left for three more meals.'

'You need more than three good meals,' said Joe. 'You all look much too thin.'

'Perhaps we are too thin, but we're better than we were,' said Jean. 'Those medicines have helped. We've had fruit, coconut milk and pig meat today, and we are clean again after washing with soap.'

'It's a strange sort of life for you,' said Joe. 'What were you all doing before the Japs came?'

'Most of us were married. Our husbands had jobs here,' said Jean.

'And now they're in prison in Singapore?' Joe asked.

'Yes. We think so,' Jean said.

'Would you like to be there as well?' asked Joe.

'Yes. It would be easier than walking from place to place,' said Jean.

'The Japs don't know what to do with you,' Joe said. 'Couldn't you stay in one place and live there until the war is over?'

'Yes, we've thought of that,' said Jean. 'But we need food and we can't pay for it.'

'No, you can't,' said Joe. After a few minutes, he looked up and said, 'I know where I can get some chickens for you.'

'But we haven't paid for the soap yet,' Jean said.

'The Japs paid for it,' said Joe. 'I stole a pair of boots from one of them and sold the boots for the soap.'

'You were lucky not to get caught,' said Jean.

'It's easy to trick[41] these Japs,' said Joe.

'Are you going to steal the chickens, too?' asked Jean. 'Please be careful.'

'We'll be all right,' said Joe. 'If you get a chicken, eat it. Don't ask where it came from.'

'All right, Joe, I won't,' Jean said.

She sat down on the ground beside Robin, and Joe sat beside her.

'Now tell me more about Australia,' she said to Joe. 'Is it very hot there?'

'Yes, it is,' Joe replied. 'Sometimes it's 47°C, but it's a very dry heat. You don't sweat like you do here, but you feel thirsty.'

'What does the country look like?' Jean asked him. She knew he liked to talk about his homeland. And she wanted to learn more about Australia.

'It's all red.' Joe told her. 'The earth and the rocks are red. At sunset, everything turns purple. It's beautiful. In the wet season, it rains and the grass makes the land green for a couple of months. Then everything turns back to red again. Where do you come from?'

'Southampton,' Jean answered.

'Where all the ships sail from?' he asked.

'Yes, that's right,' Jean said. 'It's not very beautiful, but I was happy there. I often dream of the day when I can go back and see it all again.'

They went on talking for a few minutes and then Joe got up to go.

'We can't see you tomorrow,' he said. 'We've got to leave at dawn. But we'll be back the day after.'

Jean picked up Robin and walked back with Joe to the lorries.

'We'll rest here tomorrow and walk to Pohoi the day after,' she told him.

'We'll get those chickens for you,' he said.

'Please be careful,' said Jean seriously.

'There's no danger,' replied Joe. 'If it's dangerous, we'll forget about the chickens and look for something else. I don't want to get into trouble. I want to keep safe for two years, until the end of the war, and then go home.'

'Will the war last for two more years?' asked Jean.

'That's what Ben says,' answered Joe. 'But cheer up! You'll

soon have some chickens.'

'Please be careful,' Jean said again.

'I will. Goodbye, Jean,' said Joe.

'Goodbye, Joe,' said Jean.

10

Five Black Chickens

Next morning, they heard the lorries drive away, but they did not see the Australians. The women and children rested that day and they walked on to Pohoi the day after. The two lorries passed them on the road about midday. The lorries were empty now, and heading back towards the railway. Joe and Ben waved to the women as they passed and the women waved back.

No chickens dropped from the back of the lorries and Jean was glad. She knew that the men would try hard to get the chickens. She was worried that they would be caught. They had not got the chickens, so she knew that they were safe.

That evening, when they were in the school house at Pohoi, a small Malay boy came to see them. He was carrying a green canvas sack. He said that he had been sent by a Chinese man in Gombang. Jean looked in the sack and saw five chickens. They were alive and their feet were tied.

Jean had to think of a story to tell the Japanese guards. She could not keep the chickens secret from them. She decided to ask Mrs Frith for advice.

'What can we tell the Japs, Mrs Frith?' she asked.

'They'll see us killing the birds and cooking them. We can't tell them that the Australians sent them to us. Joe and Ben are certain to have stolen them and they'll get into trouble.'

'We can say that the villagers here gave them to us,' said Mrs Frith.

'No, we can't say that,' said Jean. 'The people here aren't very friendly and the Japs wouldn't believe us. They would ask the headman and the headman wouldn't help us.'

'Can't we say that we bought them?' asked Mrs Frith.

'Yes, we can, but the Japs will ask us where we got the money,' said Jean.

'We can say we sold a brooch,' said Mrs Frith.

'I don't think they'll believe that,' said Jean. 'When we've bought things before, they've usually been with us.'

'Then we must tell them that the Australians gave us the money,' said Mrs Frith.

'All right,' said Jean sadly. 'But I don't want to get them into trouble.'

'They won't get into trouble,' said Mrs Frith. 'Nobody will know that they gave us the chickens.'

'All right,' said Jean. 'We'll say that we bought the chickens with the Australians' money. But where will we say we bought them?'

'Where did the Malay boy come from?' asked Mrs Frith.

'He came from Gombang,' replied Jean. 'We haven't got there yet so we can't say we bought them there. We'll have to say that the Australians gave us money at Berkapor. We tried to buy some chickens there, but there weren't any. Then someone said he could get us some, so we gave him the money.'

'I hope they'll believe our story, said Mrs Frith. 'We'll have to give the Japs one of the chickens. Then they won't ask too many questions, and they might help us if there's any trouble.'

'I'm not going to give them a chicken,' said Jean firmly. 'The Australians got the chickens for us, not for the Japs.'

'Yes, dear,' said Mrs Frith, 'I agree. But I think we'll have to give them one. They may even ask for two.'

Jean knew that Mrs Frith was right. She went to talk to the sergeant.

'Look,' she said. 'We have good supper tonight. We buy chickens.'

She opened the sack and showed him the chickens. Then she reached inside and pulled one out.

'This is for you,' she said and gave it to him.

The sergeant was very surprised.

'You buy?' he asked.

'Yes,' said Jean. 'Very good supper tonight.'

'Where you get money?' he asked.

'Australians gave us money. They say we too thin,' said Jean. 'Now we have good supper. One chicken for you.'

'Two,' said the sergeant.

'No,' said Jean firmly. 'One. It is a present, because you kind and help children and let us walk slowly. There are only five chickens and there are seventeen of us.'

She opened the sack and let him count them. Then she noticed that all the chickens were very big and black. They were not like the chickens they had seen in the villages.

'One for you and four for us,' she said.

The sergeant nodded his head and smiled at her. He went off happily, carrying a chicken under his arm. That night, the guards and the prisoners had a good meal of chicken and rice.

That same day, the senior Japanese officer at Kuantan was very angry. His name was Captain Sugamo. He lived in the house where the British D.C. had lived. In the garden, there were twenty, black Leghorn hens[42] which the D.C. had brought back from England in 1939. Captain Sugamo now kept them and he was very proud[43] of them. Early in the morning, he learned that

She opened the sack and showed him the chickens. Then she reached inside and pulled one out.

five of them were missing. The green sack in which their corn was kept was also missing.

Captain Sugamo called the army police. He ordered them to find the chickens and the men who had stolen them.

They immediately suspected[44] the Australian lorry drivers and went to their hut. They found some tinned food and packets of cigarettes, but there were no chickens and no green sack.

Captain Sugamo ordered the army police to look all over the town. The next day, the police went into every house and shop in Kuantan, looking for black feathers or a green sack. They found nothing.

Captain Sugamo became more and more angry. He ordered the police to inspect the houses of his own soldiers, but they still found nothing. Some of the soldiers were out of Kuantan, guarding two of the Australian lorry drivers. Next day, Captain Sugamo sent four policemen to question the soldiers and the Australians.

On the road between Pohoi and Bahat, the policemen met a group of women and children walking along the road. Two Japanese soldiers were with them and one of them had his rifle over one shoulder and a green bag over the other. The policemen stopped their jeep and asked the sergeant where he got the sack.

The sergeant pointed to Jean and the police began to question her. She told them her story. The Australians had given them some money. They had paid for some chickens at Berkapor. The chickens were brought in the green sack.

The policemen did not believe her. They asked her the same questions, again and again. Sometimes, they hit her face or kicked her legs or stamped on her feet. Jean still gave the same answers. She knew that it was a poor story and that the police did not believe it. But she could not think of anything else to say.

Two hours later, three lorries drove down the road. The driver of the second lorry was Joe Harman. The sergeant stopped him at once and brought him to the police.

'Is this the man who gave you the money?' asked the policeman.

'I've been telling them about the four dollars you gave us, Joe,' said Jean. 'We bought some chickens with the money, but they won't believe me.'

'You didn't give her money,' the policemen said. 'You gave her the chickens in this bag. You stole this bag and the chickens from the Commanding Officer at Kuantan.'

Joe looked at Jean's bleeding face and her bleeding feet. He knew at once that he must tell the truth to protect her.

'Leave her alone, you fools,' he said in a slow and angry voice. 'Yes, I stole those chickens and I gave them to her.'

Immediately, the policeman ordered the women and children to get into the lorries. They took them and Joe straight to Captain Sugamo.

Captain Sugamo decided that Joe must die. The policemen fastened Joe's hands and feet to a tree with nails. They were going to beat him to death. Captain Sugamo ordered the women and children to watch.

11

Prisoners Without a Guard

When the Japanese thought the Australian was dead, Captain Sugamo spoke to the women and children.

'You are very bad people,' he said. 'There's no place for you here. You go to Kota Bharu. You will walk, now.'

It was midday and very hot. They collected their things and set off at once on the road to the north. They wanted to leave

Kuantan as quickly as possible. Captain Sugamo also punished the Japanese sergeant. He took the other soldier away, so the sergeant was by himself and he felt very lonely.

It was now July. They left Kuantan and made their way slowly up the coast. They spent the first night at a fishing village. But they did not sleep much, because the children kept waking up. They were dreaming about Joe Harman's death and they woke up feeling frightened.

All next week, they did not have a rest day. They walked on as fast as possible, to get away from Captain Sugamo.

The east coast was beautiful and much healthier for them. Also, it was cooler, because a light wind blew in from the sea. They had fresh fish every day. Soon, they grew stronger and did not become ill so easily. Each day, they washed in the sea and the sea water helped their skin diseases.

They also found that they had more time to enjoy themselves. The children began to play, for the first time since Panong. One of the mothers started a school on their rest day, and Jean began to teach Robin how to walk.

The only person who was not happier and healthier was the Japanese sergeant. Now, he had no one to talk to and he sat by himself, looking miserable. Once or twice, Jean tried to speak to him, but he did not reply.

They walked on up the coast, stopping at fishing villages after each day's march. There were only a few Japanese army posts on the way. When they came to one, they reported to the officer and walked on. Often they did not see any soldiers for a week.

From time to time, one of the group fell sick. Then they stopped and waited until the person was better. No one else died. They began to feel that the bad days were over.

Towards the end of August, they reached Kuala Telang. This village was on a river, about seventy miles from Kota Bahru. The villagers planted rice in the fields beside the river and caught fish in nets along the beach.

The sergeant was now ill with fever. The women felt sorry for him. He had always helped to carry the children, and he had wept when any of the children died. Now he had fever and they carried his bag, his rifle and his boots. When they came into the village, one of the women was leading the sergeant by the arm. He was so ill that he did not know where he was.

Jean went to the headman by herself. He was a man of about fifty, called Mat Amin bin Taib. She told him who they were.

'We are prisoners,' she said. 'We've been sent from Kuantan to Kota Bahru. We need food and shelter. This Japanese soldier is our guard. He is ill with fever and we must find a cool house for him. Please let us stay somewhere and give us some food.'

'We have no place here where European women would like to stay,' said Mat Amin slowly.

'We don't live like European women any more,' said Jean. 'We're prisoners and we live like your women. We don't need special houses and beds. We need a floor to sleep on, and a little fish or vegetables with some rice.'

'You can have the same food as we eat,' Mat Amin said. 'But it is strange to see European women living like this.'

Mat Amin took the sergeant into his own house. He gave him some medicine for his fever and a mattress to lie on. Jean and Mrs Frith left the sergeant there and went to look after the children and cook the supper.

When they went back to the headman's house, in the morning, the sergeant was much worse. He wanted to die, and the women knew that they could not help him. Jean took the sergeant's pocket book out of his shirt. Inside it she found a photograph of a woman with four children. She

Now he had fever and they carried his bag, his rifle and his boots.

showed him the photograph. She hoped that it might make him want to fight the fever. But he made a sign to her to put it away. When Jean looked back, she saw tears on his cheeks.

The sergeant grew weaker and weaker and, after two days, he died.

They buried him in the Muslim cemetery. Most of them wept a little, because he had become a good friend.

Now they were prisoners without a guard. The women talked about what they should do.

'I don't see why we can't stay in this village,' said Mrs Frith. 'It's a nice place and there aren't any Japs near here. I would like to stay quietly here until the war is over.'

'Yes, so would I,' said Jean. 'But the Japs are certain to find us. Then the headman will get into trouble for letting us stay. The Japs might kill him.'

'But they might not find us,' said one of the mothers.

'Perhaps not,' said Jean, 'but Mat Amin will be in danger if we stay.'

'Yes, you're right,' said Mrs Frith.

'And there's another thing,' said Jean. 'The villagers will have to find food for us.'

'Why can't we grow our own food?' asked Mrs Frith. 'Half of the rice fields haven't been planted yet.'

'No, they haven't,' said Jean. 'I wonder why not.'

'All the men have been taken away by the Japs,' said one of the women. 'They're probably working on the railway that Joe spoke about.'

'Perhaps we could work in the rice fields?' said Jean.

'I couldn't do that,' said one of the women. 'I'm much too old. I couldn't walk about in mud and water and plant rice.'

'But it's a good idea,' said another woman. 'I would work in the rice fields if we could stay here, in one place.'

'I agree with you,' said Mrs Frith. 'The Japs would probably agree too. At the moment, we go from village to village and no one wants to feed us. If we stay here, we can work and grow our own food.'

After some more discussion, they all agreed that Jean should ask Mat Amin if they could stay in the village.

12

Kuala Telang

In the morning, Jean went to see Mat Amin, the headman. She found him outside his house and greeted him politely. Then she began to talk to him.

'Mat Amin, why are there so many fields without rice this year?' she asked.

'There are no men to plant the rice,' Mat Amin told her. 'The fishermen are here, but they haven't time to work in the fields. All the other men are working for the Japanese.'

'Are they working on the railway?' asked Jean.

'No,' he said. 'They are making a runway for aeroplanes at Gong Kedak.'

'Will they come back soon and plant the rice?' Jean asked.

'I don't think so,' Mat Amin replied. 'After they finish the runway at Gong Kedak, they will make one at Machang and then another at Tan Yongmat. The Japanese will keep the men for a long time.'

'Who will plant the rice, then?' asked Jean.

'The women will plant as much as they can,' said Mat Amin. 'We'll have enough rice for ourselves, but we won't have any rice to sell to the Japanese.'

'Mat Amin,' said Jean. 'I'd like to discuss something important with you. If a man was with us, I'd ask him to speak to you. But we are all women. I hope you won't be angry if I speak to you.'

Mat Amin smiled at her and led her up the steps of his house onto a verandah. They sat down on the floor, facing each other. He called his wife to bring them some coffee. While they waited, Jean spoke of other things, because that was the custom[45].

Soon, the coffee came in two thick glasses. It was without milk and sweet with sugar. Jean lifted her glass and drank a little. Then she put her glass down and began to talk to him.

'Mat Amin, we are in difficulties,' she said. 'Our guard is dead and we must decide what to do. You know what has happened to us. We were taken prisoner at Panong and, since then, we have walked hundreds of miles. The Japanese officers in the towns did not want us, so they sent us onto the next place. We have been

walking from place to place for six months and half of the group have died.'

'I know all this,' said Mat Amin.

'Our guard is now dead, so what shall we do?' asked Jean. 'We can go and find a Japanese officer, but he won't want us. If we were men, perhaps they'd shoot us quickly. But we're women and children. They'll send us away. One day, we'll come to a swampy area and die of fever.'

'Don't be afraid,' said Mat Amin. 'God sends evil things to test us. The Koran tells us this.'

Jean suddenly remembered what the headman at Dilit had said to her.

'The Koran also says that God is pleased if you are kind to women and children,' Jean told Mat Amin.

'Where does it say that?' asked the headman.

'In the fourth Surah,' Jean answered.

'Are you a Muslim?' he asked in surprise.

'No, I'm not, I'm a Christian. We are all Christians,' Jean said. 'But once, we stayed in a village where the headman was kind to us. When we thanked him, he said that to us. I don't know the Koran.'

'You're a very clever woman,' he said. 'Tell me what you want.'

'We want to stay here, in this village,' Jean said, 'and work in the fields.'

Mat Amin looked very surprised, but he did not say anything.

'Please let us stay here for two weeks,' Jean continued. 'In those two weeks, your women can show us how to plant rice. We'll work all day, in order to pay you for our food and our shelter.'

'But the Japanese will be angry if I let you stay,' said Mat Amin.

'I know that,' said Jean. 'So after two weeks, I'll go and find a Japanese officer. I'll tell him that we are planting rice. You can come with me and speak to the officer. You can tell him that the Japanese will get more rice if we stay here and work.'

'But European women don't work in rice fields,' said Mat Amin after a few moments.

'European women don't walk and die as we have done,' Jean replied.

Mat Amin was silent.

'You must decide, Mat Amin,' she said. 'You can send us away or you can help us. If you send us away, we'll die. If you help us, the British will thank you when they come back. They will come back, because many countries are fighting with them, against the Japanese.'

'I hope they come back soon,' said Mat Amin.

They sat in silence for a time, drinking their coffee slowly. After some minutes, Mat Amin spoke to Jean.

'I can't decide this quickly,' he said. 'All my people must know about your plan. I must discuss it with my brothers.'

Jean went away. That evening, she saw a group of old men at Mat Amin's house. She knew that they were talking about her plan.

Later that evening, Mat Amin came and asked for Jean. Jean went out to see him. She stood talking to him, by the light of a small oil lamp.

'I've talked to my brothers about your plan,' he told her. 'Some of the men are afraid. They think that the British will be angry, if you work in the fields. The British might say that we forced you to work.'

'We can write a letter,' said Jean. 'We'll say that we want to do the work. You can show the letter to the British, when they come.'

'You don't need to write a letter,' Mat Amin said. 'You can tell them, when they come.'

The next day, the women went to work in the fields. Two girls from the village showed them how to plant the rice. The fields were full of mud and water, but the women did not find the work too hard. At the end of two weeks, they had finished planting the rice.

On the sixteenth day, Jean and Mat Amin left the village to look for the Japanese. They took with them the sergeant's rifle, his uniform and his paybook.

The nearest Japanese soldiers were at Kuala Rakit, which was twenty-seven miles away. On the way, Jean and Mat Amin stayed with the headman of a village. When they reached Kuala Rakit, Mat Amin took Jean to the senior officer of the Malay administration. His name was Tungku Bentara Raja.

Tungku Bentara spoke very good English. When Jean told him about their long march, he was very sorry for them.

'This is terrible,' he said. 'European women mustn't work in the fields.'

'We want to plant rice,' said Jean. 'We don't want to go on walking from place to place. If the Japanese have got a camp somewhere, we'll have to go there. But if they haven't got a camp, we'd like to stay at Kuala Telang.'

'They haven't got a camp,' said Tungku Bentara. 'Perhaps they will let you stay at Kuala Telang. Tonight, you must stay at my house. Tomorrow, I'll take you both to talk with the Japanese civil administrator.'

That night Jean slept in a bed for the first time for nearly seven months. She found it very hot and she did not sleep very well.

The next morning, she went with Tungku Bentara and Mat Amin to the Japanese civil administrator. This Japanese man had been to a university in America and spoke good English.

'I'd like to help you,' he said, when Jean had told him her story. 'Unfortunately, I'm not in charge of prisoners. I'll take you to Colonel Matisika. He's the officer in charge of the army, here. He'll decide what to do with you.'

Colonel Matisika was not pleased when he heard Jean's

story. He had no camp for women prisoners. He had no soldiers to look after them.

'I can't look after these prisoners,' he said.

'Then what can they do?' asked Tungku Bentara.

'They'll have to go to Kota Bahru,' said the colonel.

'Is there a camp there?' asked the civil administrator.

'No, of course there isn't,' said Colonel Matisika.

'Then why can't they stay where they are?' asked the civil administrator.

'Because I don't want to look after them,' Colonel Matisika said. 'If they stay, you must look after them.'

'All right,' said the civil administrator. 'I'll look after them.'

As they left the office, the civil administrator spoke to Tungku Bentara. He told him that the women and children could stay where they were. Jean went back to Kuala Telang with Mat Amin.

They lived there for three years.

13

After the War

The war ended in 1945 and the British returned to Malaya. The women and children were taken from Kuala Telang to Kota Bahru, and a plane flew them to Singapore. There they met the men who had been taken away at Panong.

Jean told Bill Holland what had happened to Eileen and the two children. He listened sadly. But he still had Robin, who was now a strong little boy of four. Bill saw how much Robin liked Jean and he asked her to stay with them.

While they were in Singapore, Jean found out about her own family. Her brother, Donald, had died in Burma. He had been captured by the Japanese and sent to work on the railway, where so many prisoners died.

She sent a telegram to her mother in England. After ten days, she had a telegram from her aunt in Wales. It told her that her mother had died three years earlier. Now Jean was alone in the world.

When they arrived back in England, Bill Holland asked Jean to marry him. But she refused and went to stay with her aunt in Wales.

Later, Jean went to London. She found a job with a firm called Pack and Levy, which made leather shoes and handbags. She was the secretary to Mr Pack, the manager. Jean found a small room and began to live a quiet life, like any other English girl.

Jean often remembered the war years in Malaya. She thought about the women and children who had died on the long march and she never forgot about Joe Harman's death. Although she was only twenty-seven, she felt a lot older. She did not think about the future. Jean wanted to go on living quietly. She did not want to get married and have children.

For the next two years, Jean lived a quiet life in London. One day, she received a letter from a lawyer. An uncle who lived in Scotland had died and left[46] her some money. Jean remembered once visiting someone in Scotland, but she had forgotten about him. The letter asked her to go and see the lawyer.

The lawyer read the will to Jean and explained that her uncle had left her £53 000.

'That means that you needn't work any more, Miss Paget,' the lawyer told her. 'The income[47] from the money will be about £1000 a year. You can have a small house, a car and a servant.'

'Suddenly I seem to be rich,' Jean said.

'Yes, you're now a rich woman,' said the lawyer. 'You'll have to decide what you want to do with this money.'

'Yes, I will,' said Jean, 'but I won't decide in a hurry. For the moment, I'll go on working with Pack and Levy.'

Jean worked for two more months and then she went to see the lawyer again.

'I've decided what I want to do with some of the money,' she told him. 'I want to go to Malaya and build a well[48].'

The lawyer was very surprised. Jean had to explain to him what had happened to her during the war.

'So you see,' she said, finishing her story, 'we stayed in Kuala Telang for three years. They were happy years and the people were very kind to us. We weren't able to pay them for their kindness. But now that I have this money, I can give them a present.'

'But why give them a well?' asked the lawyer.

'The women in the village have no well,' she explained. 'They have to walk two miles to get water. Then they have to carry it two miles back. A well would make a great difference to the lives of the women. It wouldn't be very expensive.'

'So you want to go back to this village,' the lawyer said. 'And what will you do after that?'

'I don't know,' replied Jean. 'But I'll leave Pack and Levy now. When I come back, I'll look for something else to do.'

The lawyer arranged with banks in Malaya to let her have her money when she needed it. He also wrote to the D.C. at Kota Bahru, and told him that Jean was coming.

So in June, 1948, Jean set out once more for Malaya. She took with her only a very little luggage. She never returned to England.

14
The Well

The D.C. met Jean at the airport at Kota Bahru and took her back to stay at his house. She stayed in Kota Bahru for two days. Jean was surprised to find that she had become famous. People in Malaya knew what she had done during the war.

Early on the third morning, a driver took Jean to Kuala Telang in a jeep. She took with her only a small hand basket. She was dressed in Malay dress, just as she had been when she lived at the village.

The D.C. had sent a message to Mat Amin, and the village was waiting for her when she arrived. Everyone was glad to see her again and she met the men who had come back from the war. That night, she slept once again on the ground. She did not sleep well, but she felt happier than she had been in London.

Next morning, she began to discuss her plan with the women.

'When I got back to England,' she told them, 'I had no money so I had to work. I worked in an office and typed letters. One day I received a lot of money from my uncle. Now I'm rich and I don't have to work.'

She stopped speaking for a little. The women talked to one another about what she had said.

'I have come back,' Jean continued, 'because I want to give you all a present. You were so kind to us when we stayed with you. I want to give you a present that will be useful to you women. I want to build a well so that you can get water easily. I also want to build a washing house, where you can wash your clothes. Then you won't have to go to the river.'

By now, the women were very excited. She waited until they were silent again.

'I want you to decide where the well should be, and where the washing house should be,' she said. 'You must also show me what the washing house should be like inside. Then we can ask the men if they agree.'

The women discussed this plan excitedly for two hours. At first, they were afraid that the men would not agree. Jean told them that she would talk to Mat Amin. Then a few of them sat down together with Jean. They made drawings of the well and the washing house in the sand.

In the evening, Jean went to see Mat Amin. They sat together on the verandah, talking and drinking coffee.

'I want to give a present to the village,' said Jean, after a little while.

'My wife has been talking about this all day,' said Mat Amin. 'She says that you want to build a well and a washing house.'

'Yes, that's right,' Jean said. 'I know how long it takes to carry water to the village. It's very hard work for the women to carry water every day. I want to help them.'

'But the river was good enough for their mothers,' said Mat Amin. 'If the women have a well, they'll become lazy.'

'But they'll have more time and more strength to do other work and help the men,' replied Jean.

'God decrees[49] what happens to men and to women,' said Mat Amin.

'Yes, but remember that God is pleased if you are kind to women,' replied Jean.

'Yes, I remember,' said Mat Amin, smiling. 'You said these words to me many times, when you were here. I'll talk to the men about the well and the washing house. The whole village must discuss your plan carefully.'

The men held their meeting the next day. During the morning, they sent for Jean and she told them her plans. She drew pictures of the well and the washing house. She showed the men where the women wanted to build them. When the men understood everything, she left them to decide.

They did not decide quickly, because the idea was very new. It would change life in the village. But after two days they told Jean that they agreed.

Only one family could build wells in that area, and they lived in Kuantan. Jean sent them a letter, asking them to come. Then she ordered cement and bricks. While she was waiting for the well-diggers, she played with the children and helped the women with the rice harvest.

The well-diggers came after three weeks. The cement and bricks had arrived, and they began work at once. The well-diggers were an old man and his two sons. They discussed with Jean what the well should look like and where it should go. Then they began to build it carefully and skilfully.

Jean spent a lot of time watching the men work. After a few days, she asked them about the terrible thing that she had never forgotten.

'Do you remember the Japanese officer at Kuantan?' she asked the old man. 'He was called Captain Sugamo.'

'Yes,' the old man replied. 'He was a very bad man. We were glad when he went away. The next officer was better.'

'Captain Sugamo was punished after the war,' she said. 'He was executed[50], because he treated the prisoners badly on the railway in Burma.'

'I didn't know that,' said the old man, 'but I'm pleased to hear it. He did some terrible things.'

'Do you remember the things he did?' asked Jean.

'Yes. Many people were tortured[51],' the old man said.

'I saw one prisoner being tortured,' said Jean. 'He helped us when we were hungry and ill. The Japanese caught him. They hung him on a tree and put nails through his hands and feet. Then they beat him until he died.'

'I remember that,' said the old man. 'He was in hospital in Kuantan.'

'In hospital?' asked Jean in surprise. 'When was he in hospital?'

'Perhaps there were two men,' the old man said.

He called to his sons, who were working in the well below him.

'Do you remember the English soldier who was hung on a tree and beaten in the first year of the war? Did he die?' he asked.

'He wasn't English,' said one of the sons. 'He was Australian. He was beaten for stealing chickens.'

'Yes,' said the old man. 'That's right. They were black chickens. But did he die?'

'Captain Sugamo ordered his men to take the soldier down in the evening,' the son answered. 'They pulled the nails out of his hands and feet. He lived.'

15

Australia

For the first time for six years, Jean felt really happy. She had tried hard not to think about the killing of Joe Harman, but she had never forgotten it. She had liked Joe and she had always felt that she had caused his death. Ever since that terrible thing had happened, she had felt sad. When she learned that he had not died, she was full of joy.

She knew now what she wanted to do. She wanted to go to Australia, to see if Joe was all right. She remembered that he lived near a place called Alice Springs. Jean was rich now. If he was in any difficulty, she could help him.

But first the well and the washing house had to be finished.

The builders worked quickly and soon everything was ready. Everyone in the village came to watch the opening ceremony. Jean drew up the first bucket of water and took it to the washing house. When she began to wash some clothes, everyone shouted and cheered and clapped. Jean knew that the villagers were happy with her present.

Two days later, she said goodbye to her friends at the village.

'Thank you, Jean,' they all said. 'We'll never forget you.'

'And I won't forget you,' she said.

When she reached Kota Bahru, she was very tired and went straight to bed. The next morning, she told the D.C. what she had done.

'Every village will want a washing house, now,' he said. 'You have given them a good idea. But what about you? What are you going to do now?'

Jean told him about Joe Harman and her plan to go to Australia.

'I'm going to Kuantan, first,' she said. 'I may be able to find out about him from the hospital there.'

Two days later, Jean flew down to Kuantan. On the way, the pilot called her to his cabin. They were flying over Kuala Telang. He flew the plane low over the village. Jean could see the women and children running out of the huts and looking up at the plane. Then the pilot flew on and Jean went back to her seat.

In Kuantan she was lucky. She found a woman who had been a nurse in the hospital during the war.

'Oh yes, I remember him,' she told Jean. 'Joe Harman – that was his name. He was terribly ill when they brought him into the hospital. We never thought he would get better, but he did. We nursed him for four months.'

Jean drew up the first bucket of water.

'I was one of the women that Joe helped,' Jean said.

'Were you the leader of the group?' the woman asked Jean. 'He often asked about you, but nobody knew where you were.'

'What happened to him?' Jean asked.

'He was sent to Singapore as soon as he could travel,' the woman replied. 'He was able to walk with the help of sticks. I expect he's all right now. But he won't be able to carry heavy loads.'

Jean flew on to Singapore. She spent a few days planning her journey. She arranged for money to be sent to her at Alice Springs.

First, she flew to Darwin. There was a bus from Darwin to Alice Springs, right in the middle of Australia. Darwin was a very dull place. There was nothing to do and nowhere to go. The bus left two days later and she was glad to leave.

For two days, she travelled fast along the dusty road. As the bus came nearer to Alice Springs, she remembered what Joe had told her about his homeland. The earth was all red and, when the sun set, the land turned purple. At last, she arrived at Alice Springs.

Jean got off the bus at the Talbot Arms Hotel, and booked a room. After tea, she walked round the town. She walked past the bungalows with their green gardens. She walked up the main street and looked at the shops. There were two cinemas, a hairdressing shop, a good dress shop, and a milk-bar. She understood why Joe had said it was a good place. She began to feel that she would like to live there.

After supper, she began her search for Joe. She did not want everyone to know how she had met him. She told the landlady[52] of the hotel that she was looking for a relation.

'I'm going to stay with my sister in Adelaide,' she said. 'My uncle asked me to try and find Joe when I was in Alice. When my uncle last heard from him, he was working on a station near here.'

'What was his name?' the landlady asked.

She understood why Joe had said it was a good place.

'Joe Harman,' Jean answered.

'Joe Harman! Didn't he work out at Wollera?' asked the landlady.

'That's right,' said Jean. 'Do you know if he's still there?'

'No, he isn't,' said the landlady. 'He came back after the war, but he only stayed for about six months. He had been badly tortured by the Japanese. They hung him on a tree and beat him.'

'How terrible,' said Jean. 'Do you know where he is now?'

'No, I don't, but one of the men over there may know,' she said.

'Do any of you know where Joe Harman is now?' she asked.

'Yes, I do,' answered one of them. 'He went back to Queensland. He's manager of a station near the Gulf. Not far from Willstown. I think the name of the ranch is Midhurst.'

'Where's Willstown?' asked Jean.

'Near the Gulf,' the landlady told her. 'That's north-east from here, about two thousand miles.'

'How can I get there?' asked Jean.

'You can get a plane from here to Cloncurry,' the landlady said. 'They fly twice a week. Then you can get a plane from there to Willstown.'

Jean thanked her for her help. Next day, she booked a seat on the plane to Cloncurry. She sent Joe a telegram to say she was coming. She also sent a letter to her lawyer. She asked him to send some money to the bank at Willstown.

Jean had to wait two days for a plane to Cloncurry. During that time, she learned more about Alice and the country. She liked Alice and was sorry to leave.

Cloncurry was much smaller than Alice. She stayed there for two nights, before the plane left for Willstown.

Finally, she reached Willstown. There, she had a big disappointment. Joe was not there. He was not even at Midhurst. He had gone to England and would not be back for two months.

16
Joe Harman

Jean now had to decide what to do. Should she wait and see Joe? Why did she want to see him? Up to now she had wanted to make sure that he was all right. She had wanted to know if he needed any help. Now she knew that he was fit and able to work. Did she have any other reason to see him?

There was another reason. She had never met anyone that she liked as much as Joe. While she believed that Joe was dead, she did not want to get married. Now she knew that he was alive and that he was not married. She was almost certain that she wanted to be his wife.

Jean decided to wait until Joe came back from England. She planned to stay at Willstown for a few days. Then she would go on to Cairns, which was a big town on the coast.

While she stayed at Willstown, Jean learned a lot about the town and the people who lived there. There were only one hundred and forty people in Willstown. There was only one shop and one bar, which sold beer to men only. It was a dull place for women to live. There were no jobs for girls. As soon as the girls were old enough, they left, and often their families went with them. Jean knew that she could not live there happily. If she married Joe, she would want to live somewhere else.

Perhaps Joe would be willing to move. But he had a very good job as manager of Midhurst. He would not get such a good job if he went back to Alice or down to Adelaide. And he would not be so happy in another place.

Jean became very worried. She began to think that she was making a mistake. Perhaps she should go back to England. Then two things happened which made her stay.

First, she had a letter from her lawyer. He told her that Joe had been in England in order to find her. Joe had found her aunt in Wales and her aunt had given him the address of Jean's lawyer. Joe was now on his way back to Australia. He would arrive in Townsville, a town not far from Cairns, in six weeks' time.

This letter made Jean very happy. Joe had gone all the way to England to find her. Perhaps he wanted to marry her. But she was still unhappy about Willstown. She did not want to live there. She wanted to live in a town like Alice.

Then something else happened. A man came into the hotel, carrying a bundle of alligator skins[53]. Suddenly, she had an idea. Perhaps she could use her money to start a workshop in Willstown. She could make shoes out of alligator skins and sell the shoes in England. She would need several girls to make the shoes. There would be jobs for some of the girls, when they left school. Perhaps they would stay in Willstown and get married.

But the girls would need somewhere to spend their money. Perhaps she could open a milk-bar and sell ice-cream, soft drinks, fresh fruit and fresh vegetables. Willstown would then be a much better place to live in.

Jean started to make plans for a workshop and a milk-bar in Willstown. She stayed for two weeks. Then she went to Cairns and wrote three letters.

First, she wrote to Joe. She told him that she was at Cairns and wanted to see him. She sent the letter to the shipping company in Townsville. He would get it when he landed there.

The second letter was to her lawyer. She asked for £5000 of her money to build the workshop and the milk-bar.

The third letter was to Mr Pack. She told him about her plans and sent him an alligator skin. She asked him if he would sell the shoes in England and act as her agent[54].

Then she waited for Joe.

After three more weeks, she got a telegram from Joe. He was arriving at the airport the next day. She felt very excited when she went to meet him. She recognised him immediately. He had not changed much, but he walked rather stiffly.

Joe did not recognise her. In Malaya, she had always been wearing Malay dress. He did not recognise the smart young lady standing at the gate. Then Jean called to him.

'Joe,' she said, and smiled.

Then Joe recognised her and smiled back.

'Hello, Jean,' he said, 'I've been half-way round the world, looking for you.'

She laughed and said, 'Well, here I am. But let's not talk now. You go and get your luggage. I'll go and get a taxi.'

Soon they were sitting on the verandah of the hotel.

'Why did you go to England, Joe?' Jean asked him.

'I won first prize in the state lottery[55],' he said. 'That's how I got the money. Later, I was working in Townsville and I met a pilot. He was the man that flew you from Kota Bahru, at the end of the war. He told me that you weren't married.'

'Of course I wasn't,' said Jean.

'But I didn't know that,' said Joe. 'You always had a baby under your arm. I thought it must be your baby and that you were married. But what about you? Why did you come to Australia?'

Then Jean told him about Kuala Telang. She explained how she had gone back there to give the villagers a well and a washing house.

'The well-diggers told me that you had not died,' Jean said. 'Then I decided to come and see if you were all right. But tell me something. Why did Captain Sugamo order the soldiers to take you from the tree?'

'I'm not sure,' said Joe. 'He came to see me in the evening. He asked me if I wanted anything, before I died. He told me that, in Japan, a dying man must be given his last request. I told him to bring me a chicken and a bottle of beer. He went away for about an hour and then came back with some men. He had not been able to find any beer. Since he could not find any, he could not allow

He did not recognise the smart young lady standing at the gate. Then Jean called to him.

me to die. He ordered the soldiers to lift me down and take me to the hospital.'

'Joe, I'm so sorry about that terrible time,' Jean said softly. 'I'm so happy that you are well again.'

'Don't let's talk about that any more,' said Joe. 'What are you going to do now? How long are you staying?'

'I may stay for quite a long time,' said Jean slowly. 'I want to try and make Willstown into a town like Alice.'

They were married six months later.

Jean worked very hard and got the workshop started. The lawyer sent her £5000 and Mr Pack agreed to sell the shoes for her. After four months, Jean was able to send the first box of shoes to London.

The milk-bar was successful as soon as it was opened. Before the end of the year, Jean had built a swimming-pool and opened a hairdressing shop.

Jean's dream was coming true. Willstown was slowly becoming a town like Alice. After three years, the number of people in the town had risen to more than four hundred. People were talking of building a new road from Cairns and opening a hospital.

Joe worked hard on the ranch and the number of cattle rose each year. Soon he had saved enough money to buy the ranch from the owner.

Jean lived in great happiness with her husband and her children, in the country she grew to love.

Points for Understanding

1

1 Where was Jean Paget born?
2 Jean and Donald were quite ordinary children . . . but . . . there was one thing unusual about them.
   (a) What was unusual about the children?
   (b) Why was it important for them?
3 Why did the rubber company in Malaya offer Jean a job?
4 What happened in September, 1939?
5 When did Jean arrive in Malaya?
6 Jean's future seemed very certain.
   (a) What would Jean's future life be like?
   (b) What happened in 1941 which changed everything for people living in Malaya?

2

1 At first, the British people in Malaya did not change their way of life. Why not?
2 The government in Kuala Lumpur asked the women and children to leave.
   (a) Why did the government ask them to leave?
   (b) Where did the government ask them to go?
   (c) Why did Jean and many other women not leave Kuala Lumpur?
3 How were the Japanese able to move so quickly?
4 Why was Mr Merriman closing the office?
5 Singapore was 200 miles south of Kuala Lumpur. Why did Jean get on a bus going north to Batu Tasik?
6 Eileen Holland's house was in a muddle. How did Jean help her?
7 Eileen and Bill Holland had three children. What were their names and how old were they?
8 What did Bill Holland want to buy in Kuala Lumpur? Did he get what he wanted?
9 A bus was leaving Kuala Lumpur for Singapore the next morning. How were the Holland family and Jean going to get from Batu Tasik to Kuala Lumpur?
10 Where did the Japanese get to during the night? How far away were they from Batu Tasik?

3

1. How far away were Jean and the Hollands from Kuala Lumpur when the car broke down?
2. Why did they decide to walk back to the bungalow?
3. Where did the young army officer take them? What did they hope to find there?
4. Jean bought a large haversack. For how many years was she going to carry this haversack?
5. The *Osprey* came round the bend in the river and the D.C. felt a great sadness. Why?

4

1. The prisoners asked for beds and mosquito nets. What was the Japanese officer's reply?
2. Why did the prisoners feel very dirty?
3. Why did Jean and the Hollands have some food?
4. Why did the Japanese take the men away?
5. How did Jean manage to get medicine brought to the prisoners?
6. How many prisoners were left after the men had been marched away?
7. Why did Captain Yoniata hit Mrs Horsefall?
8. Why did one girl die?
9. Captain Yoniata told the prisoners that they were to go,to Singapore. How were they to get there?

5

1. Why did Jean take her shoes off?
2. Why did Mrs Horsefall and Jean tell the Japanese sergeant that they must rest the next day?
3. Captain Yoniata promised to get a lorry to take them to Kuala Lumpur. When he returned in the evening, he had bad news. What was the bad news?
4. Captain Yoniata got into his car and drove off. Did they see him again?

6

1. The Japanese guards did not know the way. How was Jean able to help them?
2. 'I can do nothing except thank you,' Jean said to the headman at Dilit. What was the headman's reply?
3. 'We were sent by Captain Yoniata,' Mrs Horsefall told Major Nemu. 'Captain Yoniata said a ship would take us to prison in Singapore.' What did Major Nemu say in reply?
4. What happened to Ben Collard?

7

1. Why did Jean become the leader of the group?
2. Jean bought a length of cloth at Port Dickson and made a sarong for herself.
   (a) Why did she need to make a new dress?
   (b) How did she feel when she wore it?
   (c) What did some of the other women do later?
3. How long had Mrs Frith lived in Malaya?
4. What did Mrs Frith think would be the best thing for them to do?
5. How far away was Kuantan?
6. Eileen Holland told Jean: 'I'm so sorry for Bill. If you see him again, tell him not to be unhappy.'
   (a) Why did Eileen say these words to Jean?
   (b) What else did Eileen ask Jean to tell Bill?
7. The women saw two white men repairing a lorry by the side of the road in Merau. How much time had passed since they were first taken prisoner by the Japanese?

8

1. 'You don't look British,' said the taller man. Why did the white man not know that Jean and the other women and children were English?
2. 'We're walking to the prison camp in Kuantan,' Jean told the white man. What did he reply?
3. The white men's names were Joe Harman and Ben Leggat.
   (a) Which country did they come from?
   (b) What were they doing in Malaya?
4. What did Joe and Ben do to the lorry so that they stayed the night at Merau?

5 Why did Joe steal three cans of petrol?
6 'Where is Alice Springs?' asked Jean. What was Joe's reply?
7 What was Joe's job in his homeland?
8 How was Joe's homeland different from England?

9

1 Why did the Japanese soldiers not take the women and children on the lorries?
2 Why did Joe loosen the nut on the petrol tank?
3 Later Joe Harman came over to talk to Jean. Who was Jean with?
4 Why did Jean ask Joe to be careful?

10

1 No chickens dropped from the back of the lorries and Jean was glad. Why was she glad?
2 A Malay boy brought Jean the chickens in a sack.
   (a) What material was the sack made of?
   (b) What colour was it?
3 Jean told Mrs Frith: 'We'll have to say that the Australians gave us money at Berkapor.' Why would they have to say that to the guards?
4 Jean noticed that the chickens were not like those in the villages. What was the difference?
5 Where had Captain Sugamo's chickens come from?
6 The next day, the police went into every house and shop in Kuantan. What two things were they looking for?
7 Why did Joe tell the Japanese the truth?
8 How was Joe Harman punished?

11

1 How did Captain Sugamo punish the Japanese guard?
2 All next week they did not have a rest day. Why did the women and children walk on as far as possible?
3 Why was it much better for the women and children on the east coast?
4 What happened to their Japanese guard?
5 The women agreed that Jean should speak to Mat Amin, the headman of Kota Bahru. What was she to ask him?

12

1 Why were so many fields not planted with rice in Kota Bahru?
2 Mat Amin spoke some words from the Koran: 'God sends evil things to test us.' How did Jean reply?
3 'But the Japanese will be angry if I let you stay,' Mat Amin told Jean. What was her reply?
4 Some of the villagers were afraid to let the English women stay in Kuala Telang and work in the rice fields.
   (a) Why were they afraid?
   (b) What did Jean offer to do?
   (c) What was Mat Amin's reply to this offer?
5 Colonel Matisika was not pleased when he heard Jean's story. Why not?
6 Who gave the women permission to stay in Kuala Telang?
7 How long did the women and children stay in Kuala Telang?

13

1 The war ended in 1945 and the British flew the women and children to Singapore.
   (a) Who did Jean meet there?
   (b) What had happened to Jean's brother, Donald, and Jean's mother?
2 Later Jean went to London and found a job there.
   (a) What was the name of the firm?
   (b) What was Jean's job?
   (c) What kind of goods did the firm make?
3 Jean often remembered the war years in Malaya. Whose death did she never forget?
4 Jean received a letter from a lawyer and she went to see him.
   (a) Who had left Jean money?
   (b) How much had she been left?
5 Jean went back to see the lawyer two months later. What did she want to do with some of the money?
6 Jean left England to go to Malaya in June, 1948. Did she ever return to England?

14

1 Why did Mat Amin think the well might be bad for the women? What was Jean's reply?
2 'He wasn't English,' said one of the well-digger's sons. 'He was Australian. He was beaten for stealing chickens.'
   (a) Who was the son talking about?
   (b) Did the man live or die?

15

1 Why did Jean decide to go to Australia?
2 What did Jean learn from the nurse in Kuantan?
3 Jean began to think that she would like to live in Alice Springs. Why?
4 Jean had a big disappointment in Midhurst. What was it?

16

1 While Jean stayed in Willstown, she learned a lot about the place.
   (a) How many people lived in Willstown?
   (b) How many shops were there?
   (c) Could women drink beer in the bar?
   (d) What happened to the girls of Willstown when they grew up?
   (e) Where would Jean want to live if she married Joe?
2 Jean began to think that she was making a mistake . . . Why?
3 Two things happened which made Jean decide to stay in Willstown.
   (a) She had a letter from her lawyer. What did she learn from this letter?
   (b) She saw a man carrying a bundle of alligator skins. What idea did they give her?
4 Jean decided to open a milk-bar.
   (a) Who needed a milk-bar in Willstown?
   (b) What would she sell in the milk-bar?
5 Why did Joe think that Jean was married?
6 Jean's dream was coming true. What was Jean's dream?

Glossary

1 ***rubber estate*** (page 5)
a large farm planted with rubber trees. A rubber plantation is the part of the farm where the rubber trees grow. The rubber from the trees is used for making things like car tyres, etc.

2 ***amah*** (page 5)
a Malayan servant who looks after the children of Europeans.

3 ***pension*** (page 6)
a sum of money paid every week or every month. Jean's mother received this pension from the Rubber Company because her husband was dead.

4 ***volunteer army*** (page 8)
the men in a volunteer army offer to fight for their country. The government does not order them to become soldiers.

5 ***KL*** (page 10)
pronounced *kay ell*. English people in Malaya talk about Kuala Lumpur by using the first letters of the name.

6 ***sentries*** (page 11)
soldiers who stand on guard to stop people moving on roads, across bridges, into buildings, etc.

7 ***mosquito net*** (page 11)
a light net which is hung over a bed. The net keeps mosquitoes away from anyone sleeping in the bed. See illustration on page 12.

8 ***verandah*** (page 11)
the outside part of a building which is covered by the roof.

9 ***adults*** (page 12)
grown-up men and women.

10 ***rim of the wheel*** (page 14)
the round, metal part of a wheel. The rubber tyre is fitted onto the rim.

11 ***District Commissioner*** (page 15)
before the Second World War, Malaya was ruled by Britain. Under British Rule, the District Commissioner was the man in charge of a number of small villages. English people usually called the District Commissioner the D.C. – pronounced *dee see*.

12 ***haversack*** (page 16)
a bag which is carried on a person's back.

13 ***lighthouse*** (page 16)
a building with a large light at the top. The lighthouse in this story is at the mouth of the river and tells seamen where the river begins.

14 ***refugees*** (page 16)
people who have had to leave their homes because of war.

15 ***broken English*** (page 17)
notice how the officer speaks English. He speaks it very badly. Bad English like this is called broken English.

16 ***shyly*** (page 19)
the little girl did not meet many strangers and she was a little afraid of Jean. To speak shyly is to speak in a way which shows you are a little afraid.

17 ***inspect*** (page 21)
to make sure everything is in order. Captain Yoniata visited the women and children every morning, to see how they were. This was his morning inspection. Inspect can also mean to search houses to find something that has been stolen – see page 54.

18 ***dysentery*** (page 22)
a sickness in the stomach. A person who has dysentery has to go to the toilet all the time.

19 ***rice ration*** (page 22)
when there is very little of something, everyone must get only a small ration. There was not much rice and the prisoners had to share it out carefully.

20 ***sergeant*** (page 24)
the lowest rank in an army is an ordinary soldier. The rank above that is *corporal*. And the next rank is *sergeant*. *Captain* is a junior officer rank and a *colonel* is a higher rank of officer.

21 ***headman*** (page 24)
the chief of the village. The headman was the most important person in the village.

22 ***mangoes*** (page 25)
large, soft fruit with a thick skin.

23 ***unconscious*** (page 25)
Mrs Collard was still alive, but she was not able to see or hear anything or to speak.

24 ***scorpion*** (page 28)
a dangerous insect with a poisonous sting in its tail. If a person is stung by a scorpion, the person may die.

25 ***Fourth Surah of the Koran*** (page 31)
The Koran (Qu'ran) is the Holy Book of all Muslims. A Surah is a division of the Koran like a chapter of a book.

26 ***stretcher*** (page 31)
a light bed on which a sick person can be carried. See the illustration on page 36.

27 ***corporal*** (page 32)
see Glossary no. 20 – *sergeant*.

28 ***brooch*** (page 32)
a piece of jewellery worn on the clothing.

29 ***Muslim*** (page 33)
a follower of the teaching of Muhammad.

30 ***starved*** (page 34)
the women and children were given so little food that they nearly died.

31 ***swamps*** (page 37)
an area of flat land where the ground is full of water and mud. Grass usually grows over the mud and covers the swamps.

32 ***bark*** (page 37)
the outside covering of a tree.

33 ***plait*** (page 38)
hair tied in a long tail. See illustration on page 39.

34 ***back axle*** (page 40)
a heavy, round piece of metal which connects the back wheels of a car or lorry to the engine.

35 ***suspicious*** (page 41)
the guard was not sure if Joe and Ben were telling the truth. He was suspicious. To suspect someone is to think they have done something wrong.

36 ***bargaining*** (page 41)
arguing about the price when buying something.

37 ***station*** (page 42)
an Australian word for a very large farm.

38 ***homesick*** (page 44)
to be homesick is to be very unhappy because you are far away from home.

39 ***leak*** (page 44)
Joe does not want the Japanese guards to know that he has stolen some petrol. He turns a nut on the petrol tank so that the petrol

will come out (leak out) slowly. The Japanese will think that all the petrol was lost in this way.

40 ***coconut plantations*** (page 46)
farms with palm trees on which coconuts grow. A coconut is a large nut with milk inside. When a coconut is growing on a palm tree, it has a thick outside covering called *copra.* Copra is used to make mats and rope.

41 ***trick*** (page 48)
to deceive or cheat someone. See Glossary no. 39 – where Joe tricks the Japanese guards by loosening the nut on the petrol tank.

42 ***Leghorn hens*** (page 52)
special kind of black chicken from England. See illustration on page 53.

43 ***proud*** (page 52)
Captain Sugamo was very proud of his Leghorn hens. He often talked about them and showed them to other Japanese officers.

44 ***suspected*** (page 54)
See Glossary no. 35 – *suspicious.*

45 ***custom*** (page 61)
the way that a group of people lives which makes them different from other people. For example, their way of greeting people, offering food and drink etc.

46 ***left*** – *left her some money* (page 66)
before he died, Jean's uncle wrote a will. A will says what a person wants done with their money after their death. In his will, Jean's uncle left her his money.

47 ***income*** (page 66)
if you keep money in a bank, the bank pays interest. Jean had a lot of money and she would be able to live on the interest. She would not need to work. The interest would be her income.

48 ***well*** (page 67)
a deep hole dug into the ground out of which people can bring up water.

49 ***decrees*** (page 69)
'God decrees' means God decides what happens to men and women.

50 ***executed*** (page 70)
Captain Sugamo had been very cruel to prisoners during the war. A court decided that he must be put to death (executed).

51 ***tortured*** (page 70)
a prisoner who is tortured has many painful things done to his body.

52 ***landlady*** (page 74)
the woman who owns and looks after a small hotel.

53 ***alligator skins*** (page 78)
an alligator is an animal which lives on the banks of rivers. Its skin is hard and strong and was used to make handbags and shoes.

54 ***agent*** (page 78)
someone who looks after the business of a company in a foreign country.

55 ***state lottery*** (page 79)
a lottery is a way of winning money by chance. In many countries, the government runs the lottery. People buy tickets for the lottery and those with the winning numbers on their tickets get the prizes.

BOOKS BY

NEVIL SHUTE

unsimplified

Beyond the Black Stump
Chequer Board
Far Country
In the Wet
Landfall
Lonely Road
Marazan
Most Secret
No Highway
Old Captivity
Omnibus: A Town Like Alice, On the Beach *and* No Highway
On the Beach
Pastoral
Pied Piper
Rainbow and the Rose
Requiem for a Wren
Round the Bend
Ruined City
Slide Rule
So Distained
Stephen Morris
Three of a Kind
A Town Like Alice
Trustee from the Toolroom
What Happened to the Corbetts

A SELECTION OF GUIDED READERS AVAILABLE AT

INTERMEDIATE LEVEL

Oliver Twist *by Charles Dickens*
The Bonetti Inheritance *by Richard Prescott*
No Comebacks *by Frederick Forsyth*
The Enchanted April *by Elizabeth Von Arnim*
The Three Strangers *by Thomas Hardy*
Shane *by Jack Schaefer*
Old Mali and the Boy *by D. R. Sherman*
Bristol Murder *by Philip Prowse*
Tales of Goha *by Leslie Caplan*
The Smuggler *by Piers Plowright*
The Pearl *by John Steinbeck*
Things Fall Apart *by Chinua Achebe*
The Woman Who Disappeared *by Philip Prowse*
The Moon is Down *by John Steinbeck*
A Town Like Alice *by Nevil Shute*
The Queen of Death *by John Milne*
Walkabout *by James Vance Marshall*
Meet Me in Istanbul *by Richard Chisholm*
The Great Gatsby *by F. Scott Fitzgerald*
The Space Invaders *by Geoffrey Matthews*
My Cousin Rachel *by Daphne du Maurier*
I'm the King of the Castle *by Susan Hill*
Dracula *by Bram Stoker*
The Sign of Four *by Sir Arthur Conan Doyle*
The Speckled Band and Other Stories by *Sir Arthur Conan Doyle*
The Eye of the Tiger *by Wilbur Smith*
The Queen of Spades and Other Stories *by Aleksandr Pushkin*
The Diamond Hunters *by Wilbur Smith*
When Rain Clouds Gather *by Bessie Head*
Banker *by Dick Francis*
No Longer at Ease *by Chinua Achebe*
The Franchise Affair *by Josephine Tey*
The Case of the Lonely Lady *by John Milne*

For further information on the full selection of Readers at all five levels in the series, please refer to the Macmillan Readers catalogue.

Published by Macmillan Heinemann ELT
Between Towns Road, Oxford OX4 3PP
Macmillan Heinemann ELT is an imprint of
Macmillan Publishers Limited
Companies and representatives throughout the world
Heinemann is a registered trademark of Harcourt Education, used under licence.

ISBN 978-1-4050-7316-5

First published by William Heinemann Ltd 1950

This retold version by D. R. Hill for Macmillan Readers
First published 1977

This edition first published 2005

Illustrated by Kay Dixey
Original cover template design by Jackie Hill
Cover photography by Corbis

Printed in Thailand

2011 2010 2009 2008 2007
10 9 8 7 6 5 4 3